RAMONA

The Novel

by

Johnny John Heinz

TF
CP

Published by Twenty First Century Publishers Ltd. in conjunction with UPSO.

Published in Great Britain, July 2002.

ISBN: 1-904433-01-4

To order additional copies of Ramona and other books by Johnny John Heinz please visit: www.twentyfirstcenturypublishers.com

RAMONA

CONTENTS

RHODODENDRON

Since long before human memory the rhododendron has reproduced each year its perfect blooms. From deep in the shade at its roots it reaches up through the foliage, bursting through to the light in a mass of colour. It climbs the mountainside, planting and layering its way ever higher. Some varieties, evicted from their Himalayan home, have reached Europe, where in the right conditions these émigrés become rampant, clambering high among the native trees of their new locality, and some claim they poison the surrounding soil for all but their species - this I do not believe, but then this book is not the story of rhododendrons....

JJH.

PROLOGUE

AN ORANGE GROVE IN SEVILLE

Ramona

Ramona did not know where she came from: she knew neither her parents nor her precise age. It was early spring in the square beside the Cathedral of Seville, the air heavy with the soft scent of orange blossom. The little girl sat among the orange trees as if daydreaming in the afternoon sun, when the uniformed police officer approached her. He had seen her earlier, too young to be alone, waiting for her parents in the Cathedral? No, too long a time by now.

She told him her name was Ramona. He guessed she was five or six years old, but she could not say where her parents were, or who was with her. He asked if she was with her older sister, her aunt, her nursemaid, only to elicit the same blank response. When he asked where she came from, she simply said it was a long way away, but she spoke with the timbre of the local Spanish. Fernando was taken with the pretty child. He held her hand as he walked with her around the square, hoping to find the desperate parents. No one. They entered the Cathedral. No one. They walked around the square again. No one. She remained quiet and dreamy, unresponsive to his questions.

Back at the police station with his new charge, this was the report that Fernando was filing, when he learnt that there had been a tragic accident earlier in the afternoon near the Cathedral. A young man and woman had been run down, fatally. They had no identification on them. Was there a connection to the young girl? While photographs were arranged to show to Ramona, Fernando took it upon himself to take her to his home to offer her the comfort of his wife and family, with this dreadful prospect looming before her.

Ramona remained withdrawn, dreamy not sullen. If she knew the man and the woman in the photographs she would not tell, but the police decided they were not the parents. Nor was there any clue to the identity of these two unfortunates. What to do now? Fernando's sister Clara was staying with him for a few days. Sister Clara was the principal of a village school in the Sierra Morena to the north of Seville. She suggested to the officials that she take Ramona up there with her, while the search for Ramona's identity went on. She asked little Ramona, if she would like to come with her into the mountains, and for the first time the little girl smiled as she shook her dark curls and asked if there would be snow.

And the paperwork? Fernando had asked, but they knew the state's bureaucracy would be benign to them, even today: their elder brother had been one of the many personal physicians who attended General Franco. The family joke was that with the scale of resources of the Spanish health service devoted to this one client, he should remain as healthy as any president of the United States. By the time Ronald Reagan tested this proposition some years later, absorbing lead bullets into his personal body space, Franco had long since a(de)scended to wherever it is that late dictators go.

Andalusia and Seville were beautiful but poor in those days, long before the World Exposition brought its glitz to the city. Sister Clara's little green Seat left the suburbs of Seville, passing vast mounds of the city's waste in open fields. Their journey took them north across the plains of the Quadalquivir River, before they ascended towards the west. Passing the town of Nerva, the green Seat chugged behind great trucks of ore through the bleak terrain of the open cast mines surrounding Rio Tinto, where metals, first zinc and later copper, have been extracted for thousands of years. From there they turned north again, into the western tip of the Sierra Morena near the border with Portugal. The road was narrow and potholed, twisting left and right as it climbed into the hills. They passed through villages, deserted for the Siesta, and eventually reached Sister Clara's village. Stone built houses lined the street, their fronts decorated with bright ceramic tiles. Sparsely wooded hills rose around the village, and the afternoon sun filtered through the trees with the welcoming glow of home for Sister Clara, her home and her school.

Clara's upbringing in a convent had equipped her for the life of a schoolteacher, but it had not trained her for marriage, and that meant, in rural Spain, sacrificing the opportunity of motherhood. Though she did not know it as they drove into the village, the little girl beside her in the car would take on the role of daughter. The days of search for Ramona's identity became weeks and then months. Finally, with the help of Franco's personal physician, little Ramona was officially assigned to the care of Sister Clara, who by this time wished for nothing more than that, the fulfilment of a dream that had grown these past months. As for Ramona, she now had an identity and a home.

The schoolhouse was a white stone building with arched windows that gave onto a courtyard, planted with three orange trees. For the village children this was their playground after school and where they would meet to play at weekends. In the corner of the courtyard Sister Clara had a desk where she would mark work and prepare for the next day, as she supervised the children at play. Often she would gaze wistfully at Ramona. How could it be that this beautiful little girl could be abandoned or lost in the middle of Seville? Who could lose this jewel? How could they lose it? Who could bear to lose it? Try as they may, her brother Fernando told her that there was still no trace, no sign, nothing. And the girl? She was less dreamy now, but it was as if time before the square beside the Cathedral was lost to her. Was it amnesia? She was very good at her schoolwork and showed no signs of trauma. Was the memory blocked off to guard against some dreadful secret? That seemed impossible to Sister Clara as she watched the little girl gaily play with her friends. With her long dark tresses, her brown eyes and dark complexion, she certainly looked local, and spoke in the local manner, although in a rather adult way. In medieval times, we would have called it a miracle, Clara said to herself, a miracle for me.

However hard she tried, Sister Clara could not stop the thought from surfacing, again and again, that she had stolen something that did not belong to her. But I have not, she would tell herself, to no avail. Twice a year it was her custom to go to Seville, in the cool of early spring and in September once the heat of the summer had passed. The first trip, September, since Ramona had arrived came due, and Ramona would come with her. Clara would extend her trip by two days and she would do her duty: she would enquire about the search for Ramona's real identity.

Sister Clara felt that they must go back to the "beginning", to the square beside the Cathedral, but she was worried lest some hidden trauma be released? Should she take this risk? How else could she jog a hidden memory? She asked Fernando to meet them by the Cathedral, as she was afraid to do this alone: she wanted his stability for the girl, and perhaps for herself too. Clara need not have worried. As they got out of the car, Ramona saw Fernando across the square, twenty metres distant. With a scream of delight, she launched herself towards him. Clara followed behind, unable to contain her tears, joy and relief mingling with the immense sadness that this little girl's affection, so keen for Fernando, was lost to her real family.

As Clara walked next to Fernando, Ramona skipped and danced in front of them, delighted by the memory of the place, perhaps? But no sign of stirrings of earlier memory. They visited the Alcazar, the great Moorish palace of Seville, pillars supporting delicate vaults, a splendour of colour, and passed through into the gardens behind. The paradise these gardens symbolised all those hundreds of years ago is still a paradise of verdant green in the parched landscape of Andalusia. Like a newly born foal, Ramona danced through the gardens, chatting to the visitors smiling at the tourists, and disappeared ahead of them. As Clara and Fernando turned onto a new path, they stopped dead in disbelief: Ramona was chatting to two young tourists, but what was unimaginable to them was that she was speaking fluent English. To Fernando it was a foreign language, but Clara's English was passable: she could recognise the clear accent, the sound of a native. This dark haired, dark skinned Spanish girl? English? After six months, how could she, Clara, not know of her English? But then why would she know, except by chance? Was this the solution to the mystery?

Such was the report Clara later gave at the police station, but it became clear that this was not the solution to the mystery, rather it served to deepen it. What could they in Seville practically do? As a practical matter the brother who was the physician had seen to it that Ramona now belonged to Clara. Did Clara not want her? She did. Then what should they, the police, do? The case was closed. Was it not better so? It was better so. Was it not best for the girl who had been abandoned? It was best. Should we open old wounds? We should not. Is she not happy? She is. The solution: Clara would learn to live with her "guilt". Surely that was best for them all. The concession to her conscience? From then on Clara read to Ramona for one hour every evening in English.

CHAPTER ONE

SIERRA MORENA

Ramona

The little green Seat wound its way up the road into the Sienna Morena, the last time it would make this journey before being consigned, several years overdue, to the great graveyard of little green Seats. For the whole journey Ramona's enthusiasm for the events of the last school term in Seville drew Clara into a world so different from her life at the village school, and held at bay the June heat and the dust of the road. For two years Ramona had been schooled in Seville, staying with her uncle Fernando during term time. Life would change yet again: at the age of seventeen she was planning for her future. She had finished school and it was the summer vacation.

The familiarity of home beckoned Ramona as they drew up beside the schoolhouse. The heat up here in the hills was less than down below on the plains, but it was still the time of siesta. First, they would rest and then she would meet her friends, the few of her age who remained in the village. Mostly work in the big city had by now beckoned, or for some of the boys, the copper mines. Clara had her new youngsters in the school, but the numbers had dwindled each year in line with the reduced opportunities for adults of working age.

Restless, Ramona walked out into the hills, knowing that this place was soon to be in the past for her, but what should she do? Where should she go? She had looked at university courses but remained undecided. Her singing teacher wanted her to follow her talents into music. Her other choice was foreign literature. In Spain or abroad, she wondered, as she ran through the list of scholarships she could apply for. What would Clara think? She would find out.

Clara's practice of reading to Ramona had survived into adolescence: the idea of a television in the household would have been anathema to Clara. That evening Ramona brought out a new book that had just been published to great acclaim. It is the work of an English professor in Cambridge, Ramona told Clara. Clara reached across to take the book and read the title page: *A Melody of Sadness by Alistair Jamolla.* Clara flicked open the book, looked back up at Ramona, and then started to read.

A Melody of Sadness - Chapter One
I curse the wealth of my family: the cause of my misfortune. What does wealth bring us but convenience: what can it take away? Everything, believe me, everything. That is my story. The story starts right here in Cambridge, where I have completed my first year as a research fellow, aged twenty-two. It starts on a Sunday morning, and to be more precise it starts in the Anchor pub in Silver Street, just a few hundred yards from my college, where I have rooms in addition to my house just outside town, and just a few hundred yards from the Graduate Centre, what we call the Grad Pad, where I have parked my car.

It is one of those Cambridge days we will always remember. The sun shines in a clear blue sky, the few students who remain will also be gone for the summer in a couple of days, and the first of the language students, many female, are arriving for their summer language courses. The adverse ratio in this university town of several men to each woman is about to reverse for the summer months, or at least to achieve a happy equilibrium as the language students pour in. Serious types like me, graduates, remain behind, for our work of course, research.

I would not embarrass myself by saying that I was humming to myself as I stepped out of the porters' lodge onto Trumpington Street, but the fact is that I was. I crossed the road and turned down Silver Street, as another one bit the dust. I walked the couple of hundred yards to the Anchor. Ahead of me was the bridge over the river Cam. Below were punts available for hire. Upstream to the left would take you out to the village of Grantchester through the meadows. Downstream took you past the backs of the colleges, under the bridges out to Magdalene Bridge. Later maybe: for now the Greene King beckoned, if not Tolly Cobold, or both - the favoured breweries. I turned left and entered the Anchor.

Even in those days you could find Australians behind the bar. This one brought me the requested pint of bitter and I relaxed against the bar.

No one I knew was there, but it was still early and the pub was about two thirds full. Later it would spill out through the doors on a fine day like this.

A magnifying glass concentrates sunlight to a point of focus, a bright spot of heat and light. Maybe this is just how I see it in retrospect, but as she came through the entrance of the bar, it was as if the whole place fell silent and focused on her. In a hand of three cards, I drew three aces from serendipity that day. Ace number one: I was alone at the bar. Ace number two: I was in her direct line of entry. Ace number three: this was her first day in Cambridge, so no one else had got to her yet. I guessed I had between three and five seconds to play my three aces, as she flashed a smile to the room at large. How is it that deep brown eyes can simultaneously spark with fire? Or combine indifference with invitation? Her complexion was southern, maybe Spanish; her wavy tresses of hair bounced on white clad shoulders as she moved towards me, white silk blouse, slim blue jeans, silver belt.

My natural, relaxed courtesy must have rescued me within the window of those few seconds, because she was accepting my offer of a drink. She asked for white wine, so I ordered her a Pimms. She made a heavily accented formal introduction of herself, Carmen followed by a succession of names that meant nothing to me then. The initial stiffness was a relief: no need to pretend to be cool.

Sharp as she may have looked, Carmen was young and naïve, a combination we may deride in the lecture theatre, but that we consider attractive in the situation of the bar of the Anchor on a fine June day: so young and naïve that I knew her life story by the time I was on my second pint of bitter. Like me, she had been orphaned at a young age and had no family to speak of. Unlike me, she had no inherited money but lived in institutions until she set out into the big wide world at the age of fifteen. She was now seventeen and had earned money in bars and restaurants (I later found out as a singer) to finance her language studies here in Cambridge. She had arrived yesterday evening and taken digs out on the Hills Road.

Pimms is conducive to acceptance of punting invitations. We walked out of the Anchor and strolled upriver to the wooden hut where they hire out punts by the hour, determining we should go downstream through the colleges. We walked down the steps and boarded one of the punts moored to the wooden landing jetty. I grasped the pole and expertly manoeuvred the punt out into midstream, under the bridge, and we were on our way. It was still early enough for punt traffic to be light. The river gleamed green as we slipped past Queen's College and could shortly make out the familiar sculpted features of King's College Chapel. Carmen sat back in the seat facing aft, with me in her field of view, as with a flick of the wrist I propelled the pole to the riverbed, thrust down and caught the pole on the rebound, driving the punt smoothly forward through the still waters, gently rippling behind us.

New passengers see how easy it is, before requesting their turn to punt; to power and direct the boat by means of the pole, dropped to the river bed to push the boat forward, and steer. As they assume their position on the wooden platform at the stern, the world seems to change, as in a dream where control of events slips away and the simplest actions lead to strange consequences. The chance of their staying dry approximates to zero, and the chance of their staying in the boat, and not the river, is not that much higher. Carmen battled the odds, as the punt circled, rammed and ostentatiously ignored her instructions transmitted to it via the pole. She stayed out of the river: not bad for a first time Spanish seventeen-year-old after a couple of glasses of Pimms.

I took over, and we moved on beneath the overhanging willows, beneath the Bridge of Sighs, past St John's College and on to Magdalene Bridge. We turned and lazily retraced our course, drifting slowly past the colleges beneath bridges lined with tourists, deftly avoiding the growing fleet of first time punters.

I said I had three aces. Well, it was the fourth ace, the last in the pack that clinched it. After dropping the punt, we wandered the short distance back to my college. My college has the advantage of being situated near the cake shop, so I picked up a creamy walnut cake and suggested we take tea in my rooms. The fourth ace simply popped out of the colour supplement of the Sunday paper lying on my table: they were selling tickets to a special rendition of Bizet's Carmen in the Earls Court Exhibition Hall in London. I did not consult Carmen. I simply excused myself while I made a phone call. Tickets were available for Thursday and I took two.

Ramona

Ramona interrupted Clara's reading.

"Clara, I don't see the melody of sadness in this, the title."

"Patience, Ramona. Perhaps this is setting the scene of what will be lost. Maybe those first words of the book are a clue, the curse on his wealth."

"But I'm enjoying it anyway, Clara. Carry on."

A Melody of Sadness

After tea we strolled down to the Grad Pad and picked up the car. It was as I dropped Carmen off at her digs that I asked her to come with me to London on Thursday. I did not know, but I thought she was thrilled, and I hoped so.

I had seen the Royal Tournament, staged by the military at Earls Court. It is a stadium rather than an opera house or theatre, but it had been specially set up for the production of Carmen. As I entered the building with my Carmen, I imagined her as fitting the bill for the central role, and the many heads turning towards us, and looking rapidly away again, confirmed me in this belief.

We took our places, the lights dimmed and the orchestra struck the first tones. We were transported to Spain, to a flamenco world, and I could not help but wonder at its effect on the girl by my side. Each time I turned to look at my Carmen during the performance, I saw a reflection of the Carmen on the stage. I saw the fire in her eyes as the stage Carmen sparked with fury. I saw tears glisten on her long dark lashes as the stage Carmen was consumed by grief. The whole opera was alive beside me. It was as we left that she told me she could sing all Carmen's roles in that opera. I laughed in half belief. But there was something more. As we drove back to Cambridge that evening I could not help but believe that our lives were about to change, and I could not help but believe that she felt the same.

Ramona

Again Ramona interrupted. "That bit's too short, Clara, if this is a romance. Also, he's too smug. He tells us how clever he is, but what about Carmen?" Clara continued to read.

A Melody of Sadness

I reflected with detachment the next day. What was I doing with a seventeen-year-old Spanish language student? How could she fit into my social life, the Cambridge dons, the academics? And this is my life. This is what I wish to do. She, a young girl with no formal training, how could she become part of this life I lead at Cambridge? All these years later, I wish I had asked her then about her own aspirations. I would have learned of her voice training from an early age, of her precocious musical talents, that she could have aspired to sing professionally in opera. Would it have helped? Would anything have changed? Probably not, but today I grasp at straws. Maybe if the best thing in our life had been delayed it would have been better, but I digress: what is done is done; she sang later and I still have all her recordings.

Suffice it to say, that my standing in both the college and the university rose rapidly. I know and I admit that having Carmen on my arm contributed more to my advancement than did my intellectual prowess in those days. We all have to make our way in life as we best can, and the truth is that Carmen, as I soon became aware, drew attention to me within the community. On Carmen's eighteenth birthday we were married, and before she was nineteen (I twenty-three) our daughter was born. A teenage mother? As far from it as you can imagine. Carmen loved our daughter, as I know she loved me. We took a maid to help, and this is when Carmen decided to take up where she had left off with her singing, her vocation, not at the expense of our daughter but to complement her. I always wanted her to sing the themes from Carmen to me, but she said they must be reserved for special occasions. I adored her Wagner and suffered her Verdi, in private. Her linguistic skill in song was never echoed in her spoken English that remained coloured by her mother tongue. We had it all.

Ramona

Clara stopped reading at the end of the first chapter.

"I think that's beautiful," she said.

"You're just a sentimental old lady who never had any kids," Ramona replied.

"No, Ramona. I mean the ability to sing as she does, and somehow I feel that is how she lives."

"That's what you feel when you sing, Clara."

"No, you do. I don't. That's the difference." Clara gave Ramona her wistful look.

Clara continued reading, starting on chapter two of *A Melody of Sadness*. Outside the light began to dim and the sounds of the night whispered to them through the open window. Clara's voice undulated with the text, and Ramona sat dreamily at her feet, letting the words of the book wash through her, living the story set so far away in the city of Cambridge.

"I'm sleepy," Clara said, as she closed the book at the end of the second chapter. "It's the long, hot drive back from Seville. Let's walk in the fresh night air."

The lady and the young girl stepped out into the cool of the late evening. The white arches of the schoolhouse gleamed in the moonlight. They crossed through the moonshade of the orange trees and out onto the village street. The ceramic faces of the houses glinted in the foreground, while darker shapes were set back among the shadows. The darkness of the hills loomed above them, but above that the blue-black sky was speckled with stars.

"I loved that chapter," Ramona said, "the story of the little girl. The life she had. I don't know it's..." - she stopped and tears formed in her eyes - "...what I didn't have."

Clara put her arm around Ramona, in the knowledge of the part of her life that she, Ramona, had lost, the life before the orange grove beside the Cathedral in Seville.

"It's what I sometimes feel, when I sing," Ramona whispered. "As if it's really there."

"Shall we stop the book, Ramona," Clara asked.

"No, please. Not that. I loved it. I love it now. The little girl." She brightened and laughed. "Just think, Clara, if we had never met." This thought no longer had a place in the conception of Clara's world.

CHAPTER TWO

CAMBRIDGE

Ramona

The next day was, of course, school as usual for Sister Clara. Ramona slept late, but in the middle of the morning she joined Clara to give the children a music lesson. Ramona played the piano and the children sang. Then Ramona sang to the children as she played the piano, and they clapped and banged their desks, laughing when she had finished. After that Clara continued with her lessons.

All afternoon Ramona went through prospectuses she had collected, scholarship application forms and books of advice, but still she drew a blank. What was right for her? She could combine the things she liked, but she knew it was better to choose, to focus, to concentrate. She remembered the advice of the German philosopher Hegel: that the young man does not wish to choose because of all the other things that the choice excludes. But you have to choose. I know that, she told herself. The luxury of choice is the misery of choice, she thought. If I could be like my friends who are good at just one thing. For them it's easy. Then she thought of the girl Carmen in the story, of how she had financed her way to her course in Cambridge, when even younger than Ramona now was. Incredible, but just a story. I suppose it does happen. Be practical, Ramona, be practical.

They ate late that evening, and relaxed, still weary from the travels of the previous day.

"Just one chapter tonight," Ramona said, and snuggled on the floor at Clara's feet. Clara began to read the third chapter.

A Melody of Sadness
It truly was a thunderbolt from the blue, unbelievable and indescribable. I have mentioned my family's wealth. It had all devolved to me, the last of the line, the only heir. I did not need it. I had my work in Cambridge. I had my aspirations. The wealth was simply locked away in trusts, in investments and in controlling stakes in the family businesses, long since professionally managed. This was not part of my life. It probably never would be. But it changed my life irreversibly. It destroyed my life through the mere fact of its existence.

It was a day you do not forget, a day you do not ever forget. Carmen called me from the house. She spoke clearly, she spoke rationally and to the point, but there was a depth of emotion in her voice, which I have never heard before or since in the voice of any man of woman. The maid had been bludgeoned into unconsciousness and our daughter was gone.

Three days later we received a ransom note with no amount specified and no instructions, just an indication of what was to come. That was the last we heard, never another whisper. We never saw our daughter again. The last birthday we celebrated was her fifth birthday, just a few months before, at our house with her little friends from kindergarten. I would have given everything we had to get her back, all that wealth of mine that was of no value to me. It was of value to someone, but that someone never came for the exchange. They never returned to us what was most valuable in the world.

For me the first chord of a melody had been struck which would run through me in the years to follow, the first jarring chord of the melody of which I write.

Ramona
Clara stopped and looked down at Ramona, on the ground by her feet. Ramona was expressionless. Then she said, " Has he given up already?"

"I don't think so," Clara replied. "Maybe it was not like that for him then. Maybe it just seems like it afterwards from what followed."

"How can it get worse?" Ramona asked.

"Not worse. Just how the emotions reverberate though him. What else is affected?"

"He has not lost everything," Ramona said.

"No, he has not lost everything," Clara agreed. She continued to read.

A Melody of Sadness

I will not dwell on *me*. I continued to work in college, my successes grew. I will not dwell on *Carmen*. She was tougher than me, and as to her singing, a young woman in her mid twenties, she was on the verge of fame. The first few months were agony, but agony can be borne: hope breathes life into you at the worst of times. It was what had changed in each of us that could not be borne. I now realise this, but I did not know then. I write this now to help with the understanding of what follows.

Carmen had always been spirited, lively, the fire of her soul reflected in her eyes. That is why she could sing the pieces of Bizet's Carmen: it was her own. In the depths of our loss, I could not tolerate her spirit, which to me was almost a betrayal, and as for Carmen, she could not live with my deep sadness, with my wounded spirit; she could not watch my blood spill out onto the floor everyday of our life. My grief devastated her as much as the loss of our daughter. She, our daughter, would not have wished this on you, Carmen would tell me. But what could I do?

Ramona

Clara stopped. "Grief affects them each differently," she said. "Carmen wants him to live to fight another day."

"He has everything he needs, except what he wants, Clara. She has had a life of having nothing, but what she made for herself. He had education, wealth. It fell into his lap."

"You're right," Clara agreed. "She suffers deeply, but must do something. She cannot sit and grieve, not for herself, not for him and not for the daughter, she would say."

Clara continued to read and the story unfolded as the seeds of dissent germinated between the author and Carmen. A deep sadness descended on the room as Clara's voice read on, and chapter three became chapter four as she read late into the night.

Ramona would normally miss breakfast, the sleep of the seventeen-year-old taking priority. This morning she was in the kitchen before Clara. She could not wait. She spoke as Clara entered the room.

"I cannot accept it," Ramona said.

"What?" Clara asked.

"That Carmen left him I can accept. It all seemed to lead to that. But without trace?"

"Was she being kind?" Clara asked.

"How?" This was not clear to Ramona.

"There was no remedy for the rift. If she killed all hope, would he recover?" Clara answered.

"I suppose that's true, Clara. Maybe he wouldn't recover, but certainly he would never recover as long as he had her, or I suppose even access to her, knew where she was."

"I think she felt the grief of each was feeding the grief of the other. So much time had elapsed, that she had given up hope of ever seeing the daughter. She went for the clean break."

"It's cruel to be kind," Ramona breathed. "She's a powerful woman."

"I think that's it."

"These last two chapters have rocked me. I've never read a book like it." Ramona looked at Clara, who nodded her assent. "Such a simple story, but the tension between them, the emotion dragged out of each of them in these last two chapters is killing me."

"Do you want me to stop reading?"

"I couldn't ask that. You must read. You must, tonight."

This was the last day of term for Clara's children. They finished at lunchtime. In the afternoon Clara planned to drive down to Rio Tinto, where she dispensed charity on behalf of the convent to support children in the mining communities that surrounded the copper mines. Ramona came with her. They would also take a fond farewell of the little green Seat and pick up the smart new car, which should not overheat and break down, and, the *coup de grace,* which had air conditioning. The last ride in their mobile oven would be down the hill, more breeze.

Clara's charity work had its inception years before Ramona appeared on the scene. Spain's wealth had grown, even during the last eleven years since Ramona had been involved. Many of the old public health issues had disappeared. The dire needs of children in miners' families racked by loss of breadwinners, through accident, prison or simply escape to a new life, was no longer a concern they handled. Particularly since Ramona came on the scene, Clara had sought to develop the talents of gifted children, to help raise them from their lot, for their own good, the good of their families, and for the benefit of the community. Clara had seen in Ramona's own spectacular talents, how these could so easily have been lost. What would have happened to Ramona, she thought, if it had not been Fernando to report events in the square beside the Cathedral?

In her early teens Ramona had taken to this work, because she loved to spend time with their charges. For her it was a world apart from the limited scope of their little village in the Sierra Morena and the games of the schoolyard. She was a child then, and she had her favourites, and she still had them now.

Maria's grandmother was eighty-three years old, and Maria was fourteen. She relied on her grandmother for everything, no other family remaining. For four years Ramona had brought music to Maria, and Maria sang from those sheets. As she entered the single room where they lived, Ramona could not help but think of Carmen in the story, *A Melody of Sadness*. Did little Carmen have a grandmother to look after her when she was fourteen? Did she have a child like Ramona to bring her music? Ramona thought not. Today she had brought sweets as well as music. It was hard to know who was more thrilled by the sweets, the child or the grandmother. This is hardship, Ramona thought, but so much less than it used to be, and again she thought of the fictitious Carmen, of how she would have lived. Clara came into the room, greeted and hugged the grandmother and the child, and then, taking Ramona with her, moved on, to work their way through the town. Clara distributed books these days in the hope that they would be read and passed on. The sight of one of her books in another person's house would give her great satisfaction. She was also glad that her job here was no longer the grave necessity it used to be, that she was now ever more a luxury item as the community's welfare grew.

In their smart new air-conditioned car, driving back up into the hills, Ramona talked about Maria.

"You know," she said to Clara, "when I look at Maria, I think of how much harder it was for Carmen."

"For who?" Clara asked.

"For Carmen in *A Melody of Sadness*."

"But she's a story, Ramona."

"It doesn't matter. Think of Carmen. As Maria, how could she have lived with him, with Alistair. The wrong person wrote the book, Clara: it should have been written by Carmen."

"By the character rather than the author," Clara laughed.

"He thought he could give everything to get his daughter back, but in the same breath he claimed his wealth was worth nothing, so what was he giving? She knew worth, Clara. She came from nothing and knew worth. Did he know the worth of his daughter? The worth of Carmen?"

"I think we have to read further, Ramona. We must read further."

But chapter five was the story of a vain search for Carmen, interviews, appeals, newspaper advertisements, money was no object, money was there: Carmen was not. They languished over chapter six and began to build their own fantasies about how chapter seven should continue. By then it was the end of the week, and Ramona returned to Seville and the summer job she had arranged. Clara planned to take her September visit to Seville a couple of months early. She knew that the days she would be spending with Ramona would grow less from now on. She was prepared for this but wanted to abstract herself gradually. In some ways she thought it would be harder for her to lose her niece or younger sister, as she thought of Ramona, than to lose a daughter-she thought of the book, *A Melody of Sadness* - but not an infant.

Whether it was *A Melody of Sadness* that influenced Ramona, or the natural choice of her research, she decided that she would like to consider reading literature at Cambridge. Her background and academic record did not match the standard requirements, but she was given a personal recommendation that compensated for that. She was invited to visit Cambridge in September and discuss the mechanics of competing for a place with her background, for entry in the following year. When Clara realised that the book had influenced Ramona was when she saw that Ramona would meet Alistair Jamolla. With her on the journey, Ramona took *A Melody of Sadness* that Clara had read to her, up to chapter six.

Ramona had never travelled abroad. When she arrived at London Gatwick, she amused herself wondering which countries Carmen had seen before she had arrived in Cambridge at the very same age as Ramona, in the book. She could not imagine herself arriving to meet the man she would marry. She could not imagine herself having sung in restaurants and bars to finance a course in the city of Cambridge. To be honest, she was worried about how she was going to find her way there. She had never been anywhere unfamiliar on her own. These were her worries before she even disembarked from the plane.

In the corridors leading to immigration, milling with strange people, panic set in, and she found herself leaning against a pillar sobbing her heart out, wishing she had stayed at home. An elderly German lady helped her through passport control and to find her luggage, after which her confidence grew. The instructions she had with her came into focus. She was able to find the train to London Victoria, to find her way to the underground station, to make the interminable journey across to the other side of London to Liverpool Street Station, to find the Cambridge train with one change at Audley End, and finally to join a taxi of four people from Cambridge station to the Blue Boar Hotel, where she had a reservation.

Ramona had planned to read on from chapter six of *A Melody of Sadness* on the plane, and then on the train, and then in the evening at the hotel. Now it was breakfast of the next day. Tomorrow she was due at the college. She was bright, alert and excited. Today, I will retrace the steps of Carmen on my first day in Cambridge, she said. It was a Sunday. It was September not June, but both months were outside term time. White blouse, blue jeans and silver belt, she said, remembering Carmen in the book. Shoes? I don't know.

From her street plan she saw she should turn left from the hotel and walk down Trumpington Street. Reaching Silver Street, to her left she saw the cake shop. It is early, she thought, I will look into the college first, before I go to the Anchor. She walked through the entrance by the porters' lodge. Just as all those years ago when she had stepped into the paradise of the Alcazar gardens in Seville, she felt she had crossed a doorway into another world, the buildings, the gardens, the creepers, the rich green lawns that she had never seen in Seville. The book came alive to her as she stepped into a world that had been graced by the Carmen of the novel. She imagined herself as Carmen on the arm of her new husband, and suddenly, she could see how it might have happened, how the story could come true. One enchanted garden seemed to lead to the next, as she moved through archways and gates. She was oblivious to whether she was just walking in circles or travelled miles, as she lost herself in the experience.

Ramona found herself back at the porters' lodge, eleven thirty, scene one. She walked along Trumpington Street, crossed and went down Silver Street. I do not know which route Carmen took, but this will do, she said to herself, as she followed Silver Street. On the left was the Anchor and she experienced the magic of reliving a fairy tale. Ahead was the bridge; below was the river, all as she knew it to be.

She pushed open the door of the Anchor, no bar but stairs up and stairs down, where should she go? She went to the upper bar where she found a group of rowdy young men to the left and ahead some Japanese tourists. She flashed a smile to the assembled crowd and moved to the bar. She felt ignored and moved through the pub. She took a place further along the bar and ordered a mineral water, looking around nervously, surprised that the young man behind the bar asked for money straight away. She paid and sipped her water. Relax, she said, and forced a smile for herself, moving across to a table in the sun by the window. Outside she could see boats on the river, a group of kayaks racing up from under the bridge to land just upstream from the Anchor. She decided to stay for at least as long as it takes to drink a glass of mineral water.

As soon as she left the pub, strangely dressed men in stripy blazers with flat straw hats, boaters, on their heads surrounded her offering boat rides. She chose one of the young men and descended to a punt, the right direction, downstream, the backs. She closed her ears to the guided tour in a New Zealand accent, and eventually told him to shut up. It was all so familiar to her from the book, and yet so foreign. It was so much less real than in the book: the characters were not there. It was just Ramona and a pole operator from New Zealand.

She did not go back to the college for tea and was not invited to a performance of Carmen at Earls Court. In fact, she had spoken to no one in a social capacity and wondered about the famous three to five seconds and the need for four trumps, but it had been fun, drinking in the atmosphere, as she wandered through the colleges. Back at the hotel, she was motivated to spend the evening reading the first six chapters of *A Melody of Sadness* that Clara had read to her, and was as moved by the story as the first time.

Everyone is nervous when their heart is set on something they want and their own performance is what counts for them to get it. Ramona was no exception as she took the familiar route down Trumpington Street the next morning. Running through her head were the literary topics she had chosen to discuss, should she have the opportunity, or create the opportunity. Her literature teachers in Seville had given her no guidance, but her music teacher had explained how to twist the conversation and had conducted role-plays with her. Ramona was dressed in a knee length black skirt and a white blouse, adequate for the warm weather, and in her case setting off well her dark wavy hair, hanging almost to her waist, while maintaining a serious, formal, Spanish air.

Not a student was in sight: tourism ruled on Trumpington Street today. She was still early, so she looked into the courtyard and onto the green lawns of a college called Corpus Christi. She wondered if this was a special religious sect. On the right was the magnificent chapel, which she recognised and had seen from the punt the day before, of Kings College.

"I am me. I will be early," she said, marching to the porters' lodge, and added a few Spanish swear words to herself to boost her confidence. She was surprised by the deference and cordiality with which she was greeted, she a mere supplicant. Unusually Mr Jamolla will not be able to come down to receive you, she was told, by reason of a knee injury. She was led through the grounds she had visited the day before, through an entrance and up a staircase. The porter knocked on the door and she was invited to enter. She thanked him profusely, and wondered whether she should give him a tip, before deciding not.

Alistair Jamolla was expecting the Spanish girl, an excellent prospect judging by her file before him. He looked forward to meeting her, out of the ordinary, clearly exceptionally talented. We should get photographs of the female candidates, he thought, displaying a politically incorrect attitude unusual for him, but then they did not get many Spanish girls for English Literature. He heard the knock on the door and mechanically invited entry.

He started involuntarily as she thanked the porter, the sound of her voice. Then the door swung open. She was framed in the doorway. He froze as he saw Carmen the first time she visited these rooms. Ramona stopped similarly frozen. A sensation welled up from deep within her, and she spoke one word.

"Papa."

The feeling was mutual, momentous, and instantaneous... and

then it was gone. *He* was stiff. *She* was formal. *She* did not know why she had spoken that word. *He* knew it was not Carmen. *Neither* knew what to say. *They* had to say something. *Each* was unaware of the other's confusion. *He* started the interview. It went nowhere. *She* ·raised the subjects she had rehearsed. *He* had not asked for them. *He* looked bland. *She* stuttered. *She* aborted. He tried to say something but could say nothing.

Ramona pulled his book from her bag and placed it on the table, a gesture that just seemed right. Again he looked at the face of Carmen, the figure of Carmen, the voice of Carmen and the movements of Carmen. This must be a trick. The age. The age was right, but it would be for a trick. What should he say, something non-committal?

"Has your mother told you about me?" he asked.

"My mother?" she was confused. "I have never known my mother." Should she say this?

"Everyone knows their mother." It came out unasked, and Carmen's child would know her mother - the child was five at the time.

"Sir, this is a literature interview."

"You produced my book. It is about a mother, a father, a child."

Her enthusiasm took over from what she had read, the second time, the previous night. "The early years of the child...so beautiful...missing for me."

"Missing?"

"Sir, I cannot say this in an interview..."

"Let's halt the interview, talk about the book, *A Melody of Sadness*."

"My...my aunt read it to me. The first six chapters."

"The first six chapters!" Exasperation.

"I read them again last night. The book rocked me then, and it does now."

"Then?" Accusatory

"Six months ago. It was more real than punting on the River Cam was yesterday."

"More real?"

"The characters were there in the book. Not yesterday. Only me, and some creep from New Zealand."

"Who is Carmen?"

"I did not know." She reached deep inside herself to what she knew was there, but did not know where. She found feeling but no fact. "Sir, I am the first interview candidate to ask this, probably in the history of the university."

"Ask."

"May we do a DNA test?"

The interview did not end with this request. After he complied, Ramona chose to sing a piece from Carmen that she rendered without music.

He had not listened to Bizet's Carmen, since his Carmen had left; he could not, but he still owned all her recordings. He played them on low volume to achieve the instrumental accompaniment, as she sang several pieces faultlessly from memory. Below the window a group of tourists and college staff gathered as the afternoon progressed. Without knowing it, Ramona was giving a concert to a group of fifty by three o'clock and more than twice that by four o'clock. They stood in silence, hearing just the voice, not the music. Only as the final refrain died away did the applause draw their attention to the open window. As he looked out at the courtyard below, he knew that the DNA test was irrelevant. But he would do it anyway, for the trust fund.

CHAPTER THREE

THE READING GROUP

The Reading Group
The reader closed the book and looked around at the group of ladies in the reading group. There was silence for a moment, as they released themselves from the world of make-believe, as the reader's voice trailed to a close and the real world resumed. Still no one spoke. They were lulled into the state the bedtime story intends to achieve, almost.

Vera spoke first, to comment on the reader's book. "Moving. Style. Sorry, I'm lost for words."

Gloria: " I loved it. But the plot!"

"The plot?" the reader asked.

"Yeah. Not credible for me. Change it. You know, coincidence. We don't like it."

"But it's me," the reader countered.

"Yeah, I know it's you, your style." Still Gloria speaking. "You wrote it, so I'm giving you editorial advice on *Romana*. It's what these groups are for."

The reader smiled. "Gloria, Ramona, "Ra", not Romana, "Ro". I'm Ramona. The book is *Ramona*. It's me, Gloria. Don't criticise the plot. It's me, Ramona."

The implication was obvious. The circle gasped, and Gloria felt for a moment very stupid, and then very privileged. She leant across and hugged Ramona, as liquid emotion expressed itself in her eyes.

This could have been the last session of the reading group for reasons that became apparent two days later. Did Ramona know? I think the answer is no. Why did it have to be so soon?

Gloria was dozing in bed when the telephone rang. She was

always sleepy in the morning. She tried to cut down on the white wine after dinner, but there was always a reason. Who the hell was this? It was Vera.

"Have you seen?"

Gloria raised herself onto her pillow. "Seen what, Vera? Sorry, been out with the dog this morning. Just got back." Gloria sank down again, duty done for the moment.

"Shall I read it?" A buoyant, chuffed, sort of voice.

"Go ahead."

"Bla, bla, bla, I quote, Gloria, and the prize for literature goes to, Gloria, you know the prize, there is only one, goes to ... are you listening, Gloria... Ramona Evans. Ramona's best-known work is *A Melody of Sadness* published under the *nom de plume* of Alistair Jamolla. The first part of her next work, *Ramona*, a trilogy, was released yesterday, and has been previewed to high acclaim. Ramona has been nominated as ... Gloria?"

"Vera, I am stunned, but I believe one hundred percent of what you say."

"Our Ramona, Gloria. Can you believe it? Our Ramona, who's reading us the first part of her new book, *Ramona!*"

"I just think about the other day, Vera. Is it true?"

***

Ramona

It was some hours later in Buenos Aires, given the time difference, before the news came though, and some time more before it was disseminated.

She was eager and enthused for the forthcoming performance as she sat in the dressing room, just a few minutes to go. A knock on the door and an envelope placed before her. She opened it deliberately, as it was her manner to do everything. A press cutting. She put it down. She called the make-up girl over for a final check up. She looked at the cutting. Literature prize. Boring. She looked again. *Nom de plume.* She saw the confusion of names and glanced again, astonished. *She* wrote the book? *My daughter* wrote the book. So it wasn't him after all. A smart little vixen. The Prize for Literature! Maybe I will make contact after all. Time to go. She picked up her trademark rose. It was in her contract, part of her show: before she went out to play the principal part of Carmen, she would parade on stage with a rose in her teeth.

***

The Reading Group
"Gloria, Gloria, Gloria," she said, and the ladies in the circle blinked, "this is not the end of our circle, just because I win a prize, sorry, *the* prize. You have not read *Ramona*. This is not the end. I was seventeen in Cambridge. How old am I now?" Ramona was not seventeen by a long way.

Vera: "So what do you want to say?"

"Yes, I did write *A Melody of Sadness,* but I wrote it for my father, and so I pretended he wrote it. And he would have written it. Do you understand? All those years he lived his own melody, the sadness of the years of loss, first me, and then Carmen. That's why I gave the book the name. But there's also the story of Ramona, the story you don't know, yet, the story I am still writing. I have never seen my mother, well, not after the initial phase."

Gloria: "Thank you, Ramona. We will all read your book. Just let me say," she looked around for agreement, "we are a literary society, not a self-help psychiatric group. I think I speak for us all."

Ramona was not intimidated. "I'm sure you do, since none of the rest of them speak. The next meeting's at my place on Wednesday the sixteenth. Come who will. But I'd like to see all of you." Ramona stood up and left.

Celebrity has an attraction, sufficient attraction that Ramona was forgiven her withering comment on the reading group's powers of self-expression. Even the self-appointed spokesman, Gloria, turned up to the next week's meeting. There was embarrassment and tension, covered by enthused discussion of *Ramona*, and then they sat down for the next stage of Ramona's reading of the new book, or as they now knew, that part which had been written to date.

"Before I start," Ramona opened, "let me just ask. You do understand why, in the book, *Ramona*, Ramona could only have read up to chapter six of *A Melody of Sadness,* by the time she met her father?"

Vera: "Thank you, Ramona. In the absence of time travel, it

is abundantly clear. If you, sorry she, wrote *A Melody of Sadness,* then all those chapters we love so well, about the father and daughter, had not yet happened."

Ramona laughed. "I'm sure you have as much a problem with that as I do. It cannot be. But remember, you have to have read both books to spot the logical flaw. So what? This is Art, ladies, Art. The fact is that the book is why Ramona went to Cambridge (even if she did write it afterwards), she did meet Jamolla, she did re-enact Carmen's first day in Cambridge and Clara did read the book to her. OK, the historical sequence may be wrong, but that's the way it seems in those few months looking back, and guess what? It's closer to the truth than the simple sequence of events. As I said, Art."

"How did you get into Cambridge?" The first question ever from the elegant, silk clad lady on the right.

"We'll come back to that." Ramona did not know how to answer that one at this stage, and continued to read them the book, *Ramona*.

Ramona

Few candidates have secured a place at Cambridge as rapidly as Ramona, deserving as the others may have been. The "interview" was in mid September, and she started there just three weeks later together with the year's intake of freshers for the Michaelmass term. It may have been hard for Clara, or maybe not; Ramona did not know, wrapped up in her new life as a Cambridge undergraduate. It was a strange life for a young girl from a village in the Sierra Morena, briefly baptised in Seville to city life. As to family life, well, how can you call it family life? A father she had never known, a mother she still did not know, a mother who had disappeared without trace, just as the daughter had, all those years ago. She called him "Alistair", just as she had called Clara "Clara". Familiar terms of address were limited in her life to just one, "uncle" as in Uncle Fernando.

Ramona took therapy in the early weeks of Cambridge life from a skilled psychiatrist. Gradually, he believed he was able to release the memories of the abduction, of life before that square where she had sat under the fragrant orange trees in Seville. The little girl, Ramona, had liked her kidnappers, who in the few days they held her treated her as her little princess. On that fateful day, the three of them had just arrived in Seville. Before seeking accommodation, they went to the centre of the city, to the Cathedral, as Ramona remembered. She recalled running away and believed that this had caused the accident. Whether she was to blame or not did not concern the therapist. What was clear to him was that the little girl's feelings of guilt had caused her to block off her earlier memories. Perhaps she had pretended not to remember what had happened at first. Be that as it may, the fact was that her earlier memories had been pushed down below the surface of consciousness. In his opinion, these memories could now progressively be released. Ramona's early life in Cambridge to the age of five would come back into focus, to the extent early memories are retained in any child. With the help of photographs of her life up to the age of five the effects of the therapy were dramatic, and this helped Ramona settle into the situation with Alistair.

On Sundays Ramona would visit Alistair at his house outside Cambridge. He would spend the morning recounting tales from her early life, but mostly he would relive the sadness of the lost years, and she bathed in his sorrow, at first. During the week they were around college and it was different. Some of the academics seemed to her like furniture, the traditional kind, not the sort you buy in Ikea: there forever, seldom thrown out, until, rickety beyond repair, they collapse. Many had known Carmen from when she was Ramona's age, and here she was, back, or so it seemed with the physical resemblance. Just as in the old days, they would see her walk through college, occasionally beside Alistair. They *knew* her but she did not know them.

The mystery of who Carmen had been began to grow in Ramona. This young girl, as young as she was, seventeen years old, had come to Cambridge on her own. Within months Carmen was married to Alistair: a life so different so foreign to Ramona, who could not imagine herself in that situation. She thought of the little girl, her friend Maria to whom she gave music, in Rio Tinto, with her beautiful voice. Was this a young Carmen? What was it about Carmen? They all say I look like her, but I've been in Cambridge for weeks and nothing has happened to me like to Carmen in the Anchor: no one has played those four aces for me.

CHAPTER FOUR

THE GOSPEL

Ramona
Ramona spent Christmas back at home with Clara in the village in
the Sierra Morena. Clara met her at Seville airport. On the journey
up to the village, just as Ramona had recounted her school terms in
Seville, she recounted her first term in Cambridge. It is the singing
more that anything that I love, she told Clara. We have a group, seven
of us, who sing in the different college chapels. Next term we will sing
in the famous chapel of King's College, and I hope to do a solo. It will
be recorded. And the literature is fun, but we do not work as hard as
we did at school. The familiar route seemed very different in the new
air-conditioned car. No longer were they stuck behind big lorries, the
fumes streaming in at their windows. Now they sped past lorries, cars,
buses, to reach the village in what seemed like no time. As they
entered the village, Ramona saw that everything had shrunk in size:
even the schoolhouse, so imposing, was smaller than Alistair's house.
Clara laughed and told her that she now finally believed Ramona had
grown into a woman.

That evening Clara suggested they read and Ramona chose the
book.

"We reached chapter six," Ramona said, "where he was searching
in vain for Carmen, spending the money, that meant nothing to him,
on the search, but to no avail. Read on Clara."

Clara opened the book, *A Melody of Sadness*, and turned the pages
until she reached the seventh chapter. She read in a low voice in the
darkness of the winter evening, just a table light beside her to light the
pages, crouched in the dim light at her feet the form of Ramona, head

raised, eyes intent on Clara as she read. She reached the end of the chapter and closed the book.

"Just that one word *Papa*. I suppose that's all she needed to say to him, but how did she know?" Clara asked.

"An ancient memory, buried deep, a face not seen for twelve years, maybe." Ramona smiled up at Clara. "It's a moving reunion."

"It is, but what happens now? What can there be between them: for him just memories of sadness, and for her incomprehension of that sadness. Perhaps we should stop here, Ramona."

"Read on, Clara, read on." Once again Clara read late into the night, with the girl at her feet.

Ramona did not come to breakfast the next morning. She did not surface until lunchtime. She looked tired, but Clara looked worse, her face drawn, darkness beneath her eyes.

"Was it so bad, Ramona?"

"What he went through with my mother, that is what he wanted to relive with me, those years of sadness, those years when I was gone. Why would I do that? I looked to the future, to what we could do, now I was there. He lived his own melody, the sadness of the years behind him. That's why I gave the book the name. I could not live this. Forget it! is what I screamed at him in my nightmares, but I was more important to him vanished, than I was to him as the inadvertently prodigal daughter. I felt for my mother. I felt for her for that time she was with him, after I disappeared. If it was like this, I know why she disappeared."

"Are you going back?"

"The book is not finished. I am going back."

"It's a beautiful book, Ramona. It's just so hard for me. Hard for me because I know you. Any other reader would love those chapters."

"That's it. Those chapters are for him. They are not for me." Ramona fixed her gaze on Clara and continued. "I don't know whether he will ever read beyond chapter six, whether I shall let him. That depends on him."

***

Unlike Clara, Alistair did not collect Ramona at the airport, that was not his style. She arrived back in Cambridge by train. From the station she took a taxi, driving out over the flat landscape to Alistair's house. The east wind held a chill in the air: no high ground between here and the Urals, they say. The sky was a clear Cambridge blue. Her thin Spanish blood left her shivering in the taxi, soon to be warmed by Alistair's traditional blazing hearth. He greeted her in his deferential style. Just as it was hard for her to imagine Carmen in Cambridge at her age, seventeen, it was hard to imagine him in that scene at the Anchor pub, the scene when he met Carmen. They sat before the fire sipping a traditional Cambridge sherry. Maybe it is this place that has changed him, she thought, doused the fire of youth.

"Have you read my Christmas present?" she asked.

"Incredible. How did you know?"

"You told me," she replied.

"I told you all that?"

"All that and more, these last few months."

"Incredible," he repeated. "It comes alive just as it was."

"It's a warning."

"A warning?"

"Alistair, exorcise the past. You relived it in me. I have written it down. The gospel according to Ramona, Saint Ramona."

"It's literature."

"Life cannot be literature, Alistair. We have to change it."

"Does it continue?" Alistair stood and replenished the sherry. He did not want to look at her as he awaited her answer, feared the answer.

"The book is incomplete. That depends…it depends on you."

"That's as far as you've written, then?"

"I did not say that."

"Can I see?"

"No, Alistair. Maybe. Not yet. Maybe never."

"It's about you?"

"No. It's about me and you. That's different." As she said this, Alistair let out a sigh and returned to his seat.

"So for the moment how it ends is with that word, *Papa*." He said in a low tone.

"The word of encounter in this case, Alistair. You have to admit that's how it was. How will it be?"

The Reading Group
The reading session had stretched well beyond its allotted time. It seemed a good place to stop, and Ramona closed the book. She sat there with the book on her knees, and there was silence in the circle. No one spoke. Eventually Vera broke the silence.

"Next week seems so far away. Can we take some with us?"

"That's not how we do it. It's a reading session and discussion, not critique," Gloria objected.

"Then let's take a vote," Ramona suggested. "But if you read it, then the next session has to be for discussion only - I don't read." Heads in the circle nodded assent. Gloria wanted a secret ballot, for some reason, maybe to avoid tension in the group. Each of them marked, folded and deposited her ballot paper. The result was unanimous. Gloria?

"I'll copy the next section and send a copy to each of you. Or email. Who's got email?" They all had email. As soon as they left, Ramona sent out the emails. The next session can be at my place, Ramona thought, but after that I am not so sure that will be safe, safe for me. Vera did not get to bed that night until 3 a.m., all consumed, left with a desire for more. She felt very adolescent as she cried herself to sleep that night, thinking of Ramona and what might have been. Another week.

But it was not another week, for Vera polled the group, who agreed, and they extracted even more from Ramona before the next session.

The elegant lady, Pam, until now so silent, started the debate.

"I went to Cambridge, Newnham. I often used to think, you know, the strange people, the twisted minds with powerful intellects, the banks of windows in the colleges, all those little rooms. Where was I?" She was losing her confidence, unused to being at the focus. "Oh yes. I used to wonder what goes on behind those windows, the stories, the scandals, the passions, I suppose."

"So what struck you about the chapters?" Gloria asked.

"Exactly that, Gloria. The unbelievable. There we had the reunion, the world put to rights, but something completely different pops out." Pam was struggling to put her thoughts into words.

"*Something completely different* as in Monty Python?"

Gloria asked to laughter.

"But that is it," Vera interjected. "The knight. The one who keeps on fighting as his limbs are lopped off. Finally, just a head is dancing around shouting its anger, Alistair and his sorrow."

"I don't think so," Gloria objected. "I liked Alistair. A victim. Ramona should have simply told him. Why didn't you, Ramona?"

"I think we'd better stick to what's in the chapters, Gloria," Ramona admonished her. "I think you might find the story develops differently from what you think."

"I take Gloria's point," Vera said. "I just wanted to step in and take control, all the time, change things. I could see what was happening, but I couldn't stop it. I wanted to throw the book down, tear it up, burn it, but I couldn't. I had to read it. I have to read on. And then I'll start again from the beginning, and just hope that this time it will be different. I know it won't."

Pam stepped back into action. "I think what I was trying to say is that there is something that's happening at the human level, something so different from what we expect, so unconventional, and all that in the conventional setting of Cambridge University life."

"It's so desperately sad, so sad when Ramona walks out on him," Vera said. "So sad, but so true. What else could she do? But that's why the book's so good. What else would you expect from a book with that title, *A Melody of Sadness?* Why else would you buy it? That's what it is."

"We're talking about *Ramona* here," Gloria corrected her. Vera looked flustered and felt very silly. God help these women, Ramona thought to herself, when they get on to the real story. And god help me. They'll tar-and-feather me if *this* already gives them offence. I had better say something.

"Vera, I feel your point is valid," Ramona said, and relieved Vera's defences from the impending assault lined up against her by Gloria, ready for combat. "There is an egocentricity to Alistair, as in us all. He is wallowing in his sadness. That made for a beautiful book in *A Melody of Sadness,* which I, if you like, wrote for him, through his eyes. In *Ramona* I'm telling the truth. That's why parts of *A Melody of Sadness* appear verbatim in *Ramona.* I'm not selling one book for the price of two, the same book twice. It's not a literary scam. I'm showing his world and then juxtaposing it against another perspective. Let's call it *real life*. You'll see yet another perspective later. Sorry, I shouldn't influence you. I'm only expanding on what Vera wanted to say." Vera thanked Ramona inwardly, and just wished that Ramona's words had been what she had wanted to say and had been able to say it. But then maybe *she* would have won the prize for literature.

Gloria was not to be outdone, and changed her tack.

"I accept that she had to leave him." Gloria glared at the assembly. "She welcomed him, she accepted him, she loved him, and all the time he just looked to the past. Sadness was his self-fulfilling prophecy, in modern jargon, a loser."

"But it was a huge sacrifice to herself." Pam was back on stage. "She gave up the chance of a Cambridge degree - unthinkable to Pam, a graduate - and became... well, I'm not sure. A writer? Well, let's read a bit further."

Now the serious literary criticism started, as they pulled out their notes and took it in turns to comment on the text, mostly on the first two of the five chapters, after which they had mostly given up note making, engrossed as they were in the story. Ramona sat listening, thinking never again, from now on I read at these sessions, or someone else reads her work. Gloria was right about the agenda for our reading group. Why did she join the others in voting for *this?* Gloria smiled to herself. It was clear to her what Ramona was thinking. She's manipulating us, she thought, and now she's suffering boredom, torture for her no doubt. Where does it go from here? Is our little group entering the danger zone? Her mind wandered: my ex-husband was a real bastard.

CHAPTER FIVE

CARMEN'S STORY

Ramona

I love Paris. I can walk to work from my hotel in the Marais, and then when all the tourists come into our tour office I tell them about what they can do, where they can go, and I change their money for them, and then at nine o'clock in the evening we are free, and we go down to the Latin Quarter and meet the students.

This is my only sad day, Sunday. I sit here on the tip of the Ile de la Cité and watch the waters of the Seine swirl past. In a moment I will walk over to Notre Dame, stand in front, observe the portals at its entrance, the gargoyles above, before I go into its dark insides where the candles burn. Then I will come back out into the bright light. I will walk to the Luxembourg gardens, see the statues, feel the gravel under my feet and the warmth of the sun above. I will walk back to the Louvre, where I like it inside because I can walk for miles, and then out into the gardens of the Tuileries, past the Orangerie on my right and on to the Place de la Concorde. I will look at my watch for the first time today, not yet lunchtime. What do I do before the evening? Roll on Monday.

I wander, I hate wandering, up the Champs-Elysées to the Etoile and branch right - I cannot believe I walk all these miles in one day - to take me right back down to the Place de la République, and just a few paces by my newly acquired Paris standards, back down to the Hotel de Ville and to my hotel. I can change, relax, i.e. get bored to death, and then make my way down to Saint Germain, where I will start this evening, where I will sing.

At home everyone knew who I was, they knew me as a child, they knew my mother, they knew my father, they knew the rest of my family. They would always say, hello Carmen, and they would laugh at my little jokes, smile, get angry, smile again, laugh. They were the sounding board of my guitar, of me, and would always react to whichever note I played, and always in the same way. Here in Paris, no one says, hello Carmen. When I say things I say at home in Spain, no one reacts as I expect. They do not react, or if they do, I do not understand them. Yes, I ask for a lemonade and the bartender gives it to me, but he does not see behind my smile, what I mean when I ask.

In three months I have learnt more than ever in my life before. I have practised being "not Carmen": I have practised being "someone else". It works. I have always loved my full long dark hair. My mother used to warn me that I looked like a prostitute and that is why men would follow me in the street. I knew she was not right, and here I am a goddess, but not if I behave like me, only if I behave like the new Carmen I have been practising. Caroline has helped me. She sits in a café and gauges reactions as I come in, and I do the same for her.

We have worked our way up the scale, as we have honed our movements, our pauses, our looks of vulnerability, our flashes of anger - we've tried them all, and it has been great fun, though in more successful moments escape has been difficult. In the end, I have a simple secret, and have left Caroline far behind: I enter with the background melody playing in my head, the melodies I sing to earn my living, and I move in tune to the feelings that arise from the melody. I let the melody flow over into my first reactions when I meet people. I would love to let it flow over into my life - no more drab Sundays on the banks of the Seine.

Another drab Sunday, but I sit outside in a café with Caroline on the Champs-Elysées, the most expensive one - we have long forgotten the economy of the price of drink, in favour of other economic advantage. The bright morning sun is diffused through the café blind above us. The crowd moves in both directions along the broad pavement beneath the canopy of trees, while traffic moves in spurts as the traffic lights change from red to green and back to red. Caroline has a friend who learnt English at a language school in Cambridge, a ratio of seven men to one woman, she tells me, men who come from the best families, men who are either rich or will be rich, but more important to us, the sort of men for us. We are mature women,

Caroline says to me, both of us knowing that at sixteen she still has a couple of months to catch me up. She tells me we need money, but I have enough money from my singing. It is April. We leave in early June.

Is this the England of Empire, as I read in books? The train to Cambridge is decrepit, the same as I know from anywhere, from Andalusia, from Morocco. Caroline laughs at me and tells me that streets paved with gold are really sewers: the gold comes to those who seek it and know how to find it, not to those who look at the pavement. In later life I remember Caroline as a philosopher, and I learnt all her lessons, although I am sure she never knew she was giving any - she would have charged me, if she had known. She has long since risen to heights of social rank far beyond me, and I know from her philosophy lessons that I should never try to reach her, nor ever could, but I still hope we may meet one day (a vain hope of lost youth).

Cambridge, a small town in the English countryside, cold even in the summer, June, but I am here with Caroline. She knows where to find what they call "digs" and we are established in our new venture. I already miss Paris, which we left this morning, but Caroline is happy, so I am happy.

This is our first day, she tells me, so we must split up, or we will not meet people. Should we not register at the language school, I ask her, but she looks at me in a strange way, and tells me, only if we have to, as if I have not understood her. I have no idea of where to go, but I do know what to do when I get there. The Anchor.

It was still early and I was hungry, so I had breakfast at a hotel in the centre of town called the Blue Boar. It is expensive for me but that does not matter as I start my new life in this strange place. I step out of the hotel and turn left down the street. I notice many beautiful buildings on my route, one looks like a huge church with lawns before it. I walk further, and then stare into the window of a cake shop, and think I will come back later; breakfast protects me against such desires for the moment. I turn through an archway into what we in Andalusia might call paradise. I wander through this place that, unbeknown to me now, I will come to know so well. My thoughts turn to Caroline; like her I must do something. I leave paradise and move on.

The river is so beautiful, with the boats lined up ready to go. I want to take a boat, but I do not know how. They have big poles, but there is no one there by the boats, so I think I will wait for the boatmen to return, and look behind me at a building that might be a restaurant or hotel. The Anchor.

I step inside and flash my smile, the smile that I have learnt will even breathe warmth into hell - the place comes alive before me, and the melody rings in my head. It is a song from Andalusia, and the bar is blue but for one glowing red spot at the bar, glowing with the charm of Andalusian warmth, convention and courtesy, an older man, I think, but I move, gently, towards him. I meet Alistair, mature, twenty-two years old.

Caroline's philosophy deserted me that afternoon, as did my Parisian *education* - I just thought I was back at home, but better. I have no memory of that time on the river, six hours, one hour, ten hours, but of him. What did I see? Where did we go? The next thing I do remember that I can recollect is the cake shop - I saw it earlier and wanted cake - because it was like living a dream. It was Caroline's dream, but it was real and it was mine. I was just here for adventure and I had captured Caroline's dream, which I would never tell Caroline, and never did.

In the dim lights of the Paris clubs, I would swing my hips while I sang, throw back my head and let my hair flow over my shoulders, as the melody flowed from me to the audience. I would stiffen my hips and strike flamenco poses, charging the room with emotion, and I was their magnetic pole. I knew what I felt as I sang, but I could only guess at what they felt. Today I felt the electricity flow through me from him. When he dropped me at my digs, I felt the whole world of hope collapse around me, and then came the Carmen proposal: Carmen, me, and more than that, the Carmen I loved and sang.

I will not speak of the Carmen Opera in London. No, perhaps I should talk of the Carmen opera in London. My thoughts swirl through my head as they did then. My thoughts? Is that what it is? At home it was me, the Carmen they knew, the Carmen who lived, well, the life of Carmen. What is it when I magnetize a concert hall as that

Carmen did on that day in London with Alistair at Earls Court? Is it Bizet, reincarnated from the dead? No, he wrote ink marks on pieces of paper, which I read. What is it when I sing his melody and captivate my audience, his audience? Caroline could tell me. As for me? I will never know. I may never know what it is, but I know what it is for me: it is living my life.

Alistair loved me and I loved Alistair. The logical consequence in those days? We married. You know why I came to Cambridge, so don't ask: he despised his wealth, but I loved it. He loved his academic life, worthier than a meal in the stomach: he did not come from Andalusia. The first problem was that he failed to instruct his lawyers correctly when we married. What belonged to Alistair belonged to Alistair, which was plenty. What belonged to me belonged to me, which was nothing. The second problem was that he was an academic in Cambridge and not a singer in Paris, so he had no idea of what I needed to spend. I earned nothing and had nothing to spend. Question: what do I spend my time doing in Cambridge?

The answer was the little girl and I loved that little girl. I loved that little girl in Cambridge more, I think, than I would ever have loved her in Andalusia, because - don't despise me - she was my choice and not my obligation, but I still would have loved her even then. I gave her everything, or she stole everything from me, whichever way you prefer to look at it. I only went back to my other love (apart from her and Alistair), singing, for the money, of which Alistair gave me none because it was unimportant, to him. I did not earn money from singing then in Cambridge: rather I trained, because I was the best and I knew it. One day I would use my talent for myself and my daughter. I knew that one day I would have to escape the prison of poverty (known to me from my childhood in Andalusia) imposed upon me in Cambridge by my rich husband through not ignorance but principle, belief, misguided belief, stupidity.

Carmen's autobiography: who wants to hear this? No matter. I will continue, because I want to, just as I sing because I want to sing, and if you don't like my melody, leave my bar (when I am poor), or my concert hall (when I am rich). I am Carmen. Shall we move on?

Alistair was impressed by my singing, or should I say astonished? I loved to sing to him and I know he loved it. At that level we were one. He would talk to me about the Opera, simply for aesthetic value, of course. What he failed, or rather refused, to recognise was the economic value of my singing, my release from a poverty he could never understand, because he had always had it all and still did. No, it was more than that: he saw wealth as a burden to be not discarded but thrust aside, and so he rejected what I could earn, because we (that is he) did not need it, nor want it.

CHAPTER SIX

ABDUCTION?

Ramona

What is fantasy? What is a dream? What would you do? Forget the last question: no one would do what I did, and yet it is so easy to do in these days of modern travel. You are in a small town in England, Cambridge, with your daughter, and you could both be in Andalusia, to meet her family she has never seen. Easy. You catch a plane.

If you ask me today why I never told Alistair about my family, I will tell you that he never asked, and that is true. Alistair was an orphan, a rich orphan, so when I told him that I had financed my own way to the Cambridge language school, he assumed I was an orphan. Why did I never contact my family? I did contact them, but I never told them what was really going on, and strange though it may seem, they never asked, but why would they? They had given me up anyway, at least until I saw sense and returned home from my strange foreign travels.

When I left Ramona with my brother Fernando in Seville, it was to me like going on holiday without your child, and then he told me that it was difficult for him and Clara was looking after her, so I did not worry about her. I never intended anything permanent, and then Alistair had never even noticed we were gone, engrossed as he was with some absurd literary project in his rooms in College. It was only after the accident with the maid, when he totally misinterpreted what I said to him on the telephone and called in the police, even before I knew, that everything spiralled out of control.

I am not telling the truth. Even now, as I tell the story, I cannot tell the truth, but I must. Yes, Alistair was right: there was kidnapping. So you want the truth? Perhaps I did embellish the story just now, but surely you can understand why I would do that. It is true that I came to Cambridge, as Caroline instructed me, as a gold digger, but I did love Alistair. The truth: I did love his position and money, and maybe him - let's say I did love him, and still do, if you like. But he wronged me: he had everything and gave me nothing. You must understand that I could have chosen anyone else, but he chose me. He chose me and gave me nothing. So what is a kidnapping? How can you kidnap your own daughter? Absurd. I was simply trying to prise from him what was my right, and the right of my daughter.

It took me little time to learn that however good a singer I may be, I was a hopeless kidnapper and extortionist. What to do? I hung on with Alistair, but I did not want to be with him, especially not since his descent into what I would describe as serial melancholia. I could not bring Ramona back without admitting what I had done, and quite frankly, I did not want her in this prison of Alistair's Cambridge life anyway. Clara loved Ramona and I missed Ramona, but I needed my new life. Why did you not go and start your new life, you may ask? Caroline could answer that for you better than I could, I think, but you want the answer from me, yet I do not wish to give you the answer. I do not wish to tell myself the answer, so I will not admit it, but I will say what the answer might be, or maybe again not. Suffice it to say, the trust funds and investments of Alistair, which he despised, were very, very large.

The Reading Group

It was Gloria who interrupted the flow of Ramona's words.

"I can't believe this. This cuts away the foundations of *A Melody of Sadness*. Alistair was her dupe. If you knew this, how could you have written the book?"

"I told you there would be another perspective," Ramona responded.

Pam: "That's life, Gloria."

Vera: "It's different, Gloria. They are different. Two cultures: poverty in Andalusia and the riches of the developed world. Ignorant of each other, poles apart."

"So you're not judging the gold digger, Vera?" Gloria asked.

"Aren't we all gold diggers? What should Carmen have

done? She said she lived her life and I think that's what she did, and in the end she protected the child, as any mother would."

"I think," Pam said, demonstrating her familiarity with Cambridge, "that it's like Alistair's replete after a good meal, and he pushes the walnut cake from Fitzbillies to one side contemptuously, while his wife and daughter, restricted to a diet of bread and water, eye it with avarice from the other side of the table."

Ramona laughed. "Pam, I assure you that I won't steal your simile from you and use it in my next award winning novel, but yes, I would say you've got the point. Alistair's fixation on what-he-has-but-does-not-want blocks out his perception of what the others need."

"It's Stalinesque," Gloria added. She too had got the point and Ramona resumed.

Ramona

That was all in my youth. It's different now. Would I behave differently today? Probably, but then today I have earned what I need in life, a successful performer, well off. I am still married to Alistair after all these years, I know, I have checked. It is not in his character to instruct his lawyers with regard to that wealth he despises, so I will still be his beneficiary, which means that one-day I may be very rich. People like me outlive them all.

My first thought, when I saw the news of the prize, was that she was a little vixen, just as I may have been described all those years ago, and she was after his money. Yes, I had read the book, but I had assumed that he had written it: after all, it was published under his name as author. I suppose I enjoyed the book: it expressed the sorrow, as was intended, but I missed the vibrancy - I would have described the Carmen performance at Earls Court, its life, its poignancy, but then I suppose that's me. The prize, you are asking, what prize? Well, *the prize*, the prize for literature of course.

The Reading Group
"Ramona," Vera exclaimed. "You cannot have known!"
"Ramona laughed again, brightly. "I didn't."
"You mean..." Pam was lost for words, as always.
"You know I'm still writing the book. Think about it. Well,

sorry, there's a section I have written, that I did not know where to insert, but I'm going to put it in earlier, in what we've already read." Ramona reached into her bag and took out a sheet of A4. "I'm putting this in:"

"It was some hours later in Buenos Aires, given the time difference, before the news came though, and some time more before it was disseminated. She was eager and enthused for the forthcoming performance as she sat in the dressing room, just a few minutes to go. A knock on the door and an envelope placed before her. She opened it deliberately, as it was her manner to do everything. A press cutting. She put it down. She called the make-up girl over for a final check up. She looked at the cutting. Literature prize. Boring. She looked again. Nom de plume. She saw the confusion of names and glanced again, astonished. She wrote the book? My daughter wrote the book. So it wasn't him after all. A smart little vixen. The Prize! Maybe I will make contact after all. Time to go. She picked up her trademark rose. It was in her contract, part of her show; before she went out to play the principal part of Carmen, she would parade on stage with a rose in her teeth."

"But I don't understand," Gloria said. "You've made contact with her, but you must have known where Carmen was all the time, if Clara was her sister."

"Gloria, let me remind you again that we should stick to the story in the book," Ramona replied. "I think I should read on."

Ramona

It was only after hearing of the prize that the book, *A Melody of Sadness*, began to take on a new significance for me with my knowledge of its real author. I began to wonder why she had contacted him and not me. I admit I had not contacted her all these years - I thought it was better that way, no emotional struggle once the initial loss was borne, Clara loved her, replaced me - but she could have reached me anytime. Why did she go to him? Did she reveal where I was? No, Alistair would not have let that pass. Alistair would have been on the first plane to Buenos Aires. I was, I am, his life. Alistair, poor blinkered Alistair, I have not needed you for years.

Originally it had been hard to obtain a copy of the book in Buenos Aires, but today it was everywhere, only in Spanish, so I bought a Spanish version. I had no idea where my old copy had gone. Why did this girl, my daughter, live, suffer and write down his sorrow? I could think of two answers: one was that the book had made her rich, especially now that she had won the prize; the other, my first thought, was that she wanted his money. Well, I doubted she would have any greater success than I had. The idea that she might have loved her lost-and-found father did not for a moment occur to me. Why should she? She had Clara, Fernando and the rest of them. What would she want with Alistair? Well, other than his money?

I have never been known for long deliberation and soul searching. After my performance the next day, I stayed late at the club, and then as I guessed with the time difference that dawn was breaking in southern Spain, I called Clara and we spoke for hours. She loved the book, but she also told me how bad it had been for Ramona with Alistair, in the end, and that Ramona had broken with him years before. You ask too much of me to make me admit this, but yes, I admit it, I was relieved, and the weight of the last thirty-six hours lifted from my shoulders, relief. As soon as I finished with Clara, who gave me the number, I was on the line to Ramona, speaking to her for the first time in twenty years, my dark haired, brown eyed, glittering, fiery jewel.

The Reading Group
Vera cut in. "After all those years, Ramona. What was it like?"

Ramona smiled at Vera, looked at Gloria and said, "Let's see what Carmen says."

Ramona
Some of you sentimental souls will have read *A Melody of Sadness* and have expectations of this telephone reunion from Buenos Aires to London after all those years; others of you, more inclined to current affairs and modern history, may expect us to discuss the Malvinas, the Falkland Islands. I jest, but it is to help you with the context, and remember I am Carmen, remember who I am. What struck me as, well almost hysterical, was that this famous authoress spoke her Spanish with a funny Andalusian intonation that came from me back

in those Cambridge days, but that I had so long ago ditched on my route to stardom.

Perhaps I flatter myself, but I think she was pleased to hear from me. How do you assess someone over the phone? I thought she combined the equanimity of Alistair with the softness of Clara, and to tell the truth, I was beginning to find the platitudes a touch mind numbing. She must be a better writer than conversationalist, I thought to myself, as she rambled on. Then I asked if she could sing. Well, I told her, it's my call, my cost, so sing to me, sing whatever you want. And then she sang a beautiful rendition of Carmen, which is when my tears came, so I told her I would call tomorrow for another song, and I hung up.

In London Ramona put the phone down in astonishment. Without further thought she called Clara.

"Can you guess who I just spoke to, Clara?"

"I don't need to guess. I gave her your number." Clara smiled to herself in her quiet way.

"Why did she call? She left you and the family years ago. Why call me?" Bewilderment.

"Didn't she tell you?" Clara was sure she would not have, but asked anyway.

"She didn't listen to what I was saying, at least that's what I thought, and then she asked me to sing, so I sang."

"I half wondered whether it was a hoax, by someone who had read the book," Clara said. "Now I know it wasn't. That's Carmen. Sing to her like I read to you all those years, Ramona. She'll love it."

The Reading Group

Again it was Gloria who cut in. "Are we supposed to think Carmen's some kind of musical prodigy who lives on UHF while we live on MW?"

"I think you're a bit out of date, Gloria," Pam said. "We're going digital."

"You know what I mean. Is this some kind of subplot, Ramona?" Gloria asked.

"I've thought long and hard about this, Gloria. If all Ramona did was sing to Carmen, how would she have managed to get Carmen's side of the story? You have just heard Carmen's side of the story, right? So there must be more to it." With her answer, Ramona smiled at the group.

Vera: "We await the next session with bated breath, Ramona."

"Don't hold your breath though," Ramona suggested.

"What do you mean?"

"What I mean is that I think our literary group here should take an extended break from Ramona, after all it is a trilogy. Let's look at something else. Gloria? Pam? Anyone?"

Gloria: "I vote we continue with Ramona for now." Nodding heads.

Ramona: "Not possible."

Vera: "Why ever not?"

Ramona: "I've read to you everything I have written so far." Deep gloom descended on the room, and the group decided to break for the summer. In fact, Ramona had read to them less than half of what she had written. She just did not know if she had the courage to go through with it, with them.

CHAPTER SEVEN

NOM DE PLUME

The Reading Group
The restaurant was conservatory style, built into the courtyard at the back of the hotel, Scandinavian tables, space and light. Gloria was sipping a white onion soup, while Vera daintily carved her pâté wishing she had ordered the soup; Pam had abstained for the first course and was greedily eyeing both, but still proud of her decision.

Gloria had thought out her game plan, which was to launch the subject after once again chatting about their favourite book for the moment, *A Melody of Sadness.* They each had their different opinions, but shared the view that the book struck deep to the core. It was time to strike.

"I've been thinking," Gloria said, "and bear with me. This is going to take a bit of explaining."

"Shoot," instructed Pam.

"Just a couple of weeks ago we thought that *Melody* was written by the father, right?" The other two nodded confirmation. "Then we learn that it was written by the daughter, our very own Ramona. In fact, she points it out to us, when I tell her the plot of *Ramona* is unrealistic."

"Very moving," Vera chipped in.

"Moving, yes, but does it change our perception of the book, I mean it's all about the father telling his sad story? Now we learn he didn't write it." Gloria waited for their response.

"Not for me really," Pam replied. "The book's the book."

"OK, hold off on that for the moment, but the next thing is, and she points it out to us, that in *Ramona* there's a logical impossibility, a circularity let's say: Clara reads *Melody* to Ramona, which leads Ramona to Cambridge to the unexpected reunion with the writer who turns out to be her father, but then it's Ramona who writes *Melody* so it can't have happened. It's like the Escher picture where the water flows down four stories in the mill and ends up where it started." Gloria raised her hand to stop interruption, sipping another spoon of soup. "Let me continue. She says, I mean what Ramona tells us, is that you wouldn't know, unless you read both books, but that's not true. You would know if you had *written* both books." Gloria looked around triumphantly, only to see blank return stares.

"OK, you don't get it, so let me tell you the next thing. The next thing is we discover that the little girl was never really kidnapped to start with. I admit the father didn't know this, but consider the following: one, it was her uncle who picked her up in Seville; two, she was brought up by her aunt; and three, there was never a problem for her to find her father. How does that compare to the opening scene in Seville when Ramona sits under the orange trees, that beautiful, moving scene of the poor little girl? Now let me spell it out. In books and in the real world, things happen in the past and in the present and these things that have happened or are happening determine the course of the future. Do you see what Ramona's doing? She's turning this on its head. As we go forward into the future in the book *Ramona*, the past changes to conform to the future when the future happens. It's all the wrong way round."

Vera laughed, and choked on her pâté. "Gloria I think I *have* got it now. You're amazing." Pam still looked blank, so Vera continued, "It's like me, when I'm twenty-five years old, introducing my mother to my father, because they've never met before and I think they'd make a good match, but then how come I was born? *That* can only happen *after* I've prompted the coupling of father and mother."

"Exactly," Gloria affirmed. "Like I spend all afternoon burning the autumn leaves I've raked up in my garden, and then I notice that I don't have any trees, so I can't have had any leaves, so I might as well have not bothered, and that's what I'm beginning to think about *A Melody of Sadness.*"

"Gloria! A book's a book," Pam repeated. Don't get so uptight."

"I'm not uptight, and it's not that simple. Why's she reading this book to us?"

"Because she's a member of the group," Pam responded.

. "No, Pam. It's more than that. I think she's manipulating us, but I'm not quite sure how. It's sinister. Is she playing at being god or something?"

"Why would she do that? Gloria, come on." Vera did not like this tone, and Gloria, realising this, backtracked.

"Sorry, that's not quite the word. Somehow I feel experimented on, the laboratory mouse, you know, the way she picked her moment to let us know she was Ramona and all that. And she got the prize, so *someone* knew she wrote *Melody*, but she hadn't let on to us. Anyway, enough for today. But think about it. Let's see what happens."

The main course, a mackerel delicacy, chose just the right moment to arrive at the table, and for the time being literary discussion was relegated to a subservient position. As the mackerel retreated from the foreground, it was replaced by the subject of ex-husbands, Gloria's favourite, as it allowed her to employ language not normally appropriate in polite circles. After they paid the bill, Gloria played her trump card.

"You know what we're going to do one day. We're going to ask her to sing to us." She laughed. "And that's before we reach the point in the story where her father turns out to be the world's greatest opera singer and he was doing the singing all along and not Carmen after all."

"Well, we'll have to wait for that," Vera said, to defuse Gloria's attempted pyrotechnics. "She told me she was withdrawing to concentrate on *Ramona* for as long as it takes."

***

Ramona

"Hello, Alistair." She had chosen her position in the college, so that she was silhouetted in the archway against the evening light behind. He could see a shape before him, lost in his thoughts, leaving his rooms for the week, to spend the next two days at his house just outside Cambridge. For a moment he did not react, and then he recognised her. Long gone were the days of the Anchor, the days of sadness recorded in his daughter's book.

"Hello, Carmen," he said, after more than fifteen years. "How's Ramona?"

"Alistair?"

"You wouldn't be here, if you had not seen Ramona. Come on, Carmen."

Carmen laughed and started to sing. It echoed over the college lawns and then she stopped.

"If only you had *known* me then, Alistair, and I had *known* you."

"Then we would have had nothing, Carmen. I have no regrets. We had everything. In the book it says, *we had it all.* You're not going to tell me you don't believe the book, Carmen."

"The book never interested me, Alistair. Yes, I read it in English, and then again in Spanish, after the prize. It was boring, for me."

"The truth, the beauty, the sorrow, boring?" Alistair looked at her in mock horror.

"That's the book, but you just had to pick up the phone, Alistair. You were too proud."

"And my daughter?" He asked.

"Yes, too proud for that. I thought you would fall down at my feet this evening, Alistair."

"An ageing superstar, opera singer, yes, many would."

"Do old people still go to the pub, Alistair?"

"To live nostalgia?" He asked.

"To have a drink and talk. The Anchor?" Her invitation.

She moved to his side and took his arm, hoping he would acquiesce and he did. As they reached the Anchor, Carmen said she would prefer to walk along the river to Grantchester. They walked down Laundress Lane, crossed the river and set out on the opposite bank to the Garden House Hotel.

"Whose idea was it to publish under your name," she asked, to break the silence. "It fooled me."

"It's a long story, Carmen, so I won't tell it. What I will say is that my actions were more in your character than in mine. She wouldn't show me the book, well, not beyond chapter six, so I stole it, published it (not difficult for a professor of English literature), and thought, sue me if you dare, Ramona."

Carmen laughed her deep laugh. " And she did? I mean, sue you."

"We reached an accommodation. My name became her *nom de plume.* And I signed an agreement to keep this secret. It was only when they came to award the prize, that I insisted the truth be known."

"Your career could not afford fraud on that scale?" She asked, even though she knew the answer. He knew and did not answer. She asked him to put an arm around her and he acquiesced for the second time that evening.

"I can say it in one sentence, Alistair. I should not admit this, not to you, but you are the only person I'll admit it to, the last to hear this, but the only one. Do you want to hear?"

"Fire away, Carmen, fire away," Alistair said in a false, resigned tone with a sigh, by now desperate to hear what she had to say.

"It is true that I was in love, Alistair, and it's true that I loved the child, but I was a teenager, a singer who needed her life, and I left to find that life, knowing Clara would be a better mother - pregnant pause - and that is all behind me."

"Is that all?" He asked, his tone signifying his full understanding of the proposition.

Carmen stopped, turning to face him, and very gently said, "That is everything. I hope you listened to me. I am still a young woman, little more than forty."

Alistair had easily maintained his distance, emotionally detached, up until that point. Now she pierced his calloused shell, hardened by those years of whatever he may have felt, whether as recorded in the book or otherwise.

***

I have always known that my natural parents were still married and over all those years of separation had never divorced. I had not minded: my family was Clara, Uncle Fernando and all the rest of my cousins, as defined in the widest sense. I suppose it was the Carmen in me that made me contact my father, a rich man, I knew, and also influential - I wanted to do the best for myself. It worked, in that he arranged for me to come to Cambridge, but I was incensed when he stole my book and published it before it was even finished. That crippled an already stunted relationship between father and daughter. I felt cheated, duped, a laughing stock, and rushed - I now think foolishly - home, turning my back on both him and Cambridge; I was simply too young to deal with this. Today I question if, without him, the book would have ever been published.

I did not know what to do, and it was Clara (who else?) who arranged everything, with the result that I had a steady stream of income from the highly successful sales of the book under my *nom de plume*. I have written volumes of short stories, which I may publish one day, but it was only later that I undertook to write this book, *Ramona*. It has been so much more difficult to write than *A Melody of Sadness*, quite simply because the facts are *wrong* and I have to sculpt them into shape as the work progresses. Each time I seek to edit the earlier chapters, I find that I cannot unwrite what I have written, because I cannot destroy the aesthetic truth of those words.

The stupid singing programme with my mother in Buenos Aires over the phone lasted about three weeks, because she wasn't my type. I could see why she left home: she did not fit in with us. The truth is that people in Andalusia are not all flamenco dancing Carmens: they are people like me, Clara, Fernando and, of course, little Maria, who is now big Maria and my best friend. After I returned from Cambridge, her grandmother died and she moved in with me and Clara, and then with me when I moved to Seville and later London.

Maria could not understand my rage. She had never seen me like this and it frightened her when I flew out of the flat in Knightsbridge and ran screaming into Hyde Park. When she caught me up later, and I calmed down, I could not understand it either, but it was there, and I think it will be there forever, somewhere, this rage. They had not told me, they had not bothered to tell me, they had not cared to tell me: my mother and my father were living together again in Cambridge. They had moved together weeks before. Why should I worry? I never felt rejected before, but now I did, as if they had stolen something from me that belonged to me. How can they? How can these two people be family without me, without asking me, without telling me, without considering me, without...well, without? My rage resumed. I ranted and raved that I would never ever have anything to do with them again, that I would never see them again, that they would suffer for this insult. I was brought back to the park, the trees, the military horses riding round the perimeter by Maria's laughter, not hysterical, but the laughter that follows a good joke. But Ramona, she told me, you don't have anything to do with them anyway, so what's the difference? Cold logic can be a salve to emotional hysterics and in this case it was, to be taken once every four hours for as long I live I wondered, incredulous at my own rage.

Why have I introduced this subject, so private, so personal, so embarrassing? I can only guess that the flow of this text has a power of its own to draw this from me, and because of what comes later. Clara, please help me.

Contrary to Maria's statement that I had nothing to do with them, they did contact me just four weeks later. I was calm now, most of the time. My reaction to their news was also calm - well let us just say my first reaction - I simply told Maria their news, and then I added that my only hope was that they would not call her Ramona.

The Reading Group

They had hardly started, but somehow the session came to a halt, the first meeting Ramona had joined after so many months. Vera looked across at Gloria and Gloria felt acutely embarrassed. She remained silent. It was practical Pam who moved in.

"I can understand why it has been so many months, Romana," and immediately Pam felt like an imbecile, with the possible interpretation of what she had said. Vera came to the rescue, deliberately, perhaps over-deliberately, staying with the text.

"I can see that Ramona may have experienced exclusion from her natural family situation... she did live with them for five years, early experience, you know, that kind of stuff."

"And she was an only child," Pam added, "in both situations, I mean, at home and then with Clara."

Ramona smiled at them. "No one needs exoneration. This is a story of relationships that derive from and are influenced by their own special circumstances. Let us remain humble before the power, the truth, of humankind. Shall I continue?"

Ramona

Maria looked at me with the intensity of a sinner standing before the Devil himself, a sinner claiming it could all be explained, there was some mistake somewhere, it must have been someone else, a mix-up.

Now I thought she would explode, but she dissolved in sadness. She told me to remember those days when I had visited her in Rio Tinto and many other things. Suddenly, this little girl Maria, the singer, whom I had pulled out of her misery, with my music sheets and sweets, was my mentor. This will be your sister, she told me, and in that instant I realised that this thought had not even occurred to me, my sister. I had never had a sister before. Now I would have a sister. My rage burnt white hot.

CHAPTER EIGHT

MARIA'S STORY

Ramona

I grew up with my grandmother and for all of my childhood that I can remember just the two of us lived in that little house on the edge of Rio Tinto. She was eighty-five when she died, but I now know that she had been an old woman for many years before that, all the years that I knew her. Why she had moved close to the mines of Rio Tinto is a forgotten mystery, for she had lost interest in her life after the age of twenty-five by her later years, by the time I was mothered by her, when she would relate tales to me, Maria, of those early days, constantly.

I suppose she brought me up as her mother had brought her up, which was the way she, in turn, had been brought up, maybe by her grandmother. This explains a lot about me, a living anachronism, I sometimes think I was. Many are inspired by the old gipsy way of life, flamenco in the woods, fierce women fighting with knives to win a man, castanets; but for them it is a charming fairy tale, while for me it is laced into the tapestry of my childhood, mixed in with the life of the peasantry, life on the land, again incongruous with my childhood reality among the urban (mining town) poor. Perhaps all these strands were plaited together in me, and if so, they all had one thing in common, nothing to do with the modern world in which we live.

Everyone else had family but we did not, and our isolation was probably made worse by my grandmother's interminable, repetitious stories, which grew worse with her disease. The greatest excitement in her life was when Sister Clara would bring sweets for me and we would share them. I think Sister Clara realised this and would leave me double rations. At that time the very idea that I should ever live with Clara was beyond my wildest imagination, but then I suppose that would never have happened if Ramona had not returned from Cambridge. Then, at that time, Ramona and I were so far apart in years - I was fifteen - now we are so close in years, less than three years apart. But much more than the years separated us then: Clara and Ramona descended to us from Mount Olympus. And it was Mount Olympus, compared to the life I had and the little I knew, but I had, of course, no conception of their little village in the Sierra Morena, of Seville, of London.

I have no doubt that Clara was motivated by charity and her natural kindness, but I also have no doubt that Clara brought me to live with them to solve the problem of Ramona, the post-Cambridge Ramona, who needed something more in her life than the village school, teaching, had to offer. The development of me and my talents, which I neither knew I had then nor now, was that something. It was like a role reversal from those very first days. I would relate to Ramona the tales from my grandmother, which I knew by heart, and Ramona would write them down as short stories to be read by Clara to Ramona and me in the evenings. Charming, for a couple of months, but then we were rescued by the move to Seville, where I for the first time learned the meaning of the word education, and that is why we moved to London, Ramona and I, when she accompanied me "to look after me" as I commenced at London University, where I graduated two years ago. How much of life can be squeezed into a paragraph, a paragraph in which I too ascended to Mount Olympus, by now a fully paid up member of the demigods, looking for promotion.

I cannot say it was ever family life to me, but then I suppose that is something neither I nor Ramona has ever really had, in the conventional sense. Anyway, from the age of fourteen it was my interests which lead me on, and I suppose, with time, it is true to say that Ramona and I have become the best of friends. She encourages me in what I do, and I still give her the plots for all her stories. Knowing her as I do, I have never seen her as an artist, but more of a technician: she constructs the stories from the pieces I give her. She knows my point of view and accepts it because she knows it is true. She has taken down, virtually verbatim, whole texts I have spoken on the subject, and I have the suspicion that she may even include part of this in her new book, *Ramona,* simply to cock a snook at the world, now that she has won the prize.

So what is the problem you may wonder, when everything is hunky dory (note how I attempt, often unsuccessfully, to clad my anachronistic being with a modern veneer) and we live in clover? I think you may have guessed the problem: Ramona. Why can she not escape this past that has nothing to do with her past life, her present life, or her future? Forget it, Ramona, forget it, and leave them be, as they you, I tell her. What has it got to do with you, with me, with Clara, with anyone? They live in a different soap opera, not in ours, not even in a parallel universe, more distant than that not even tangential, forget! Forget!!! The concept of "forget it", of course, does not necessarily include the inheritance, which I would certainly not advise anyone to forget, if they had the remotest chance of getting their hands on it.

Ramona is not an emotional type by any stretch of the imagination. She is, in my view, and I think her own, a bit of a plodder, even if a talented one, although this is disguised by her engaging social manner and exceptional looks. So it was an extraordinary outburst, for her, when she learnt about her natural parents moving back together: Ramona rushing out into the park screaming! You must be joking, but she did; I am the athlete in our household but I could not catch her until she was halfway to Kensington Gardens. Bystanders must have assumed we were training for the Fun Run, but I am not sure what they thought about the hysterical shrieking.

And then within a month the real news: they are to have a child. This has had a powerful effect on Ramona that I do not really understand, and I am worried for her. What do I do?

***

If the scene at the Anchor had led you to believe that both Carmen and Alistair lived in a world dedicated to first impressions, you would not be wrong. Maybe that is why she was a performer, who made her living by creating illusion on stage, in her appearances during a performance, those minutes when she would be on stage, and why she and Caroline used to practise their entries into the cafés of Paris. Maybe that was why Alistair was a professor of literature, for reasons that a professor of literature may be better qualified to answer.

Whether it was really a first impression, or came alive later, Carmen saw Maria step through the garden gate of their Cambridgeshire home as a figure from Maria's grandmother's tales, stepping into the clearing from the dark forest to shout her defiance at the soldiers guarding her imprisoned lover. In fact, Maria had come to see Alistair and Carmen with the principal intention of having them invite Ramona to be a godmother when the time came. Maria thought that "inclusion" was the solution for Ramona, but then she had not met Carmen before today.

Ramona was never intended to be a book about singers, and certainly not opera singers, but both the real world and fate (if the two are compatible) conspire against the best of intentions. As he drove into the driveway Alistair could hear a familiar female duet echoing across the lawns, but it was unfamiliar in that it contained the familiar voice of Carmen who had no partner for duets.

Alistair walked across the lawn from his redbrick garage, shorter than taking the serpentine stone path. The privacy of the house would be afforded in due course by a beech hedge he had planted, but now he could see his neighbours who had stopped their game of croquet to stroll up to the border and listen to the impromptu concert. Alistair walked across to them, a painter and his flamboyant wife, a daughter and son-in-law, both Cambridge academics. Jules, the painter was laughing as he spoke to Alistair.

"I wouldn't like to be in your shoes, old boy," he said. "Whoever she is, from what we've heard this afternoon, she's at least as good as Carmen."

"Are you suggesting my wife's a bitch?" Alistair grinned. The two of them had an understanding about how to keep their respective wives under control.

"Just a woman, Alistair."

"Well to the extent that any woman could be a bitch, Carmen would not wish to be considered less able than any other, but no, one thing I will say for her is that she just loves the music and will do anything to improve it. There's no spirit of competition in that department. I believe she would give up a role if she thought there were a better singer. So, no, I think, if this girl's so good, I'm a lucky man, for a change." The painter's wife was surprised by his tone.

"I have to give it to you, Alistair," she said, "you do rank at the top of the smarmy bastard league table."

"If both of us weren't married, I'd take that as an invitation to dance," Alistair said, "but come in anyway and join us for a drink."

They parted the beech hedge, stepped through and the five of them strolled across the lawn to the house.

Alistair had built onto the west side of the house a conservatory the height of two storeys, and attached to the house at the upper level within the conservatory was a gallery. Carmen had chosen this as her stage for tonight, so the audience settled into rattan sofas of floral design, among the plants below, all very Alcazar in its way. They sipped chilled white Valdepenas wine to enhance the authenticity of the performance, but not a word was spoken among them, capable of being spoken among them, as the two women swayed and flowed above them with the music and their voices combined and then complemented in successive roles, breaking in waves across the conservatory.

Carmen staged three curtain calls for Maria to the applause from below and ushered her down the curving staircase to join the audience. As they stepped off the bottom step, the world of opera above retreated to wherever it is that it lives while the real world takes over. Carmen was in her gardening clothes and Maria was turned out for the occasion she had planned, not for an operatic dress rehearsal.

"Alistair," Carmen enthused, "Ramona's friend Maria has come to see us." Neither of them had the vaguest idea that Ramona had a friend called Maria. Alistair proceeded to introduce Maria to the painter and his wife, while the daughter and son-in-law took an overdue leave to meet their planned evening engagements.

The painter took pains to be honest in his opinions, and the opportunity to test Alistair's probity.

"Carmen, I have admired you more than any other singer and am honoured to be your neighbour, if I could just paint with your art, but today you have been surpassed by Maria."

Carmen beamed at him.

"I could never have told Maria that. She wouldn't have believed me. I have never sung with anyone like Maria. Not because she's technically perfect, she isn't, how could she be without years of training? But the quality! Believe me, Maria, this man *does* know how to paint. You have just, deservedly, received the highest praise you could earn."

Maria accepted her demigod status with grace, but was for the moment more concerned about her mission, thought she had probably made a step in the right direction. If only the painter would go, she could get on with it. But the painter did not go before the second bottle of Valdepenas was finished, and Maria had to start worrying about train schedules. To hell with it, she said to herself, I am here for this, and if need be I'll walk the streets tonight until the first train tomorrow. Her concerns were set aside by Alistair.

"Stay here tonight, Maria. It's unpleasant to travel back to London so late, the tube at the other end and all that. I should have been home much earlier; it's my turn to cook. I'm going to start now, so one extra is easy. Agreed?"

"Agreed."

"Then chat with Carmen while I disappear in the kitchen. It's not often we entertain Ramona's friends," i.e. never.

After a joint operatic performance small talk does not come naturally, and the impromptu performance had not generated a professional post mortem, so Maria came straight to the point.

"Ramona does not know I'm here," - Carmen did not appear surprised - "If she did, my ears would be burning, white hot."

"I think I understand," Carmen responded cautiously.

"I had one intention when I came here tonight, now I have two." Maria was clear about what she wanted.

"Tell me the first," Carmen proposed, uncorking a sorely needed Valdepenas.

"Make her a goddaughter."

"Absolutely, but why do *you* tell me?" Carmen looked at Maria with interest.

"Because she's burning up, Carmen, about the sister six months hence. It's absurd, but that's how it is. Include her." Maria had stated her demand. Carmen was impassive.

"And the second?"

"Again in the interests of inclusion, not exclusion, Alistair should make a financial settlement on Ramona. I only thought of this while we were singing up there, you know, for age twenty-five or whatever."

Carmen let out the deep belly laugh of the trained opera singer.

"Maria, none of this would ever have happened if it were not for Alistair's miserly possession of his hated wealth. I agree to demand number one, but you ask him about demand two over dinner, I want to be there - I can't miss this, not this." A repeat of the operatic belly laugh.

Alistair produced fried blood sausage, boiled turnips, chopped raw cabbage in olive oil, hot green chillies and boiled white rice. Maria enjoyed it, wondering nonetheless whether he might be making a point about the cooking, but then she did not know what it was that Carmen produced when she was on the rota. Alistair was enamoured of the godmother idea, especially once Maria had explained her rationale.

"So that's settled," Alistair declaimed, voluble and clearly pleased.

"I had another thought," Maria added. "You know, some sort of financial settlement to reflect her age."

Alistair turned serious.

"Maria," he said, looking very stern, "I went through so much. Ramona went through so much. It could never be paid for."

"That's not what I'm suggesting," Maria chipped in merrily.

"You don't understand. I could never do a pay-off like that. This was my daughter, my life, my daughter's life."

"That's not what I'm saying. I'm just saying, include her in the -family, spread the wealth a bit, show she's part of the game-plan."

"Maria, I have never, never ever attached value to wealth, material wealth. I would not for one moment demean my daughter by assuming her opinion was any different. That is final."

Carmen smiled at Maria and asked, "Shall we talk about opera now?"

But Maria turned back to Alistair.

"You are absolutely wrong, Alistair. The money has no value, apart from convenience, other than the extreme value you give it, the extreme *no-value* value. Think about it Alistair, but let's not discuss it tonight. Let me just ask if the bartender in the Anchor, on that famous day when you met Carmen, would have accepted no payment for your three pints of bitter and two Pimms, in lieu of white wine, on the basis that material wealth had no value. Get real."

She would have stood up and left, except that Carmen was smiling and Alistair clearly had not the least idea of what she was talking about. She was beginning to understand what it was that Carmen had intimated to her earlier, and why Carmen wished to witness the discussion. Then she turned to Carmen with her sweetest of smiles.

"You know, this was the most wonderful evening, earlier. You were the most wonderful hosts, earlier. I was so glad to be here, earlier. But, you know what? It stinks, and I think I understand why. Maybe I can help Ramona after all."

"I hope you can. Alistair, are we having digestifs? Come on let's go back to the conservatory."

At this moment Maria realised she could not fault Carmen. Carmen had returned to Alistair and knew how to handle it, and she also realised that Carmen respected her, Maria, for more than her singing.

CHAPTER NINE

THE PROJECT

Ramona

From the third floor window of a stucco fronted mansion flat, overlooking gardens just south of Hyde Park echoed a voice.

"Maria! I cannot believe you did that!" It was mid morning, trees rustling gently in the square, and the chug of a black cab heading for Knightsbridge. Maria had just returned from Cambridge and her more measured response could not be heard in the square below. Without warning she had launched straight into the godmother scenario, and Ramona, unscripted, had reacted with utter dismay. The flat itself had two bedrooms overlooking the rear of the property, a third bedroom converted into a large Spanish kitchen, a dining room to the front and next to it a drawing room, where the two ladies sat on golden velvet sofas, facing one another over a wrought iron coffee table topped with clear glass. Ramona had calmed down after the initial shock, but there was more (worse or better?) to come.

"Do you realise, Ramona, that since you were five, you have never been in the presence of both your parents at once?"

"Maria..." A warning tone, a you-had-better-not-have-done-what-I-think-you've-done tone. Maria laughed and airily said, "I think I'll say no more for the moment." There was no need to say more.

Maria had anticipated resistance from Ramona to the idea of a reunion, so she had decided just to hint at it for the time being. In due course, she would spring it on Ramona. Her thoughts were moving towards her own agenda; slowly her ideas were forming. She was beginning to see how Carmen could fit into her plans, and then she had a flash of inspiration of how Alistair fitted into her plans, changing everything, making the impossible possible. The question was how to handle it, and the Ramona issue dropped a couple of rungs down the priority list.

Maria felt she had clearly understood the issue of Alistair's relationship to his wealth. They had all gone about it the wrong way before by addressing Alistair, when they should have been addressing his advisors. Alistair's advisors had to be making a fortune out of him, she surmised, so they would wish to keep him sweet. That meant that if they believed it was in their interests to accommodate someone close to Alistair, then they would do so, provided the business was kosher, and they were not to know, she hoped, that any such accommodation was immaterial to Alistair. Therefore, she would research her project to develop her business proposal meticulously. I believe, I can sell the concept to Carmen, Maria thought, and then it should be plain sailing to push a good business plan past the advisors, particularly if she could get to them socially as well. She was aware of her "social skills", which, she thought, I know how to use, just as Carmen did, and Ramona, who may be more beautiful than I, does not.

And what of Ramona? That problem would best be dealt with sooner rather than later, and maybe Clara's help was needed there. It was time she and Ramona paid Clara a visit, as dutiful "daughters", and she preferred to limit London life to sessions of a couple of months at most - if just to escape the air of the city and the English weather - and then she was Spanish and felt Spanish, rather than part of the cosmopolitan mix of central London.

Ramona came back into the room with a tray of olives and jamon, seated herself opposite Maria and invited her to eat, but Ramona had a ponderous expression.

"Look at your situation another way, Ramona," Maria suggested. "Next time you see a little baby in a push chair in the street, look at it, and ask yourself, does this little creature deserve my wrath?"

"That's not what I was thinking of, Maria. I was thinking about you and Carmen. You know I think Carmen's still here with you now, even though you have left her in Cambridge. And that's after just one meeting."

I will not tell her my plan, Maria thought, not yet, and took an olive. She smiled at Ramona.

"One for the pigeons," she said, flicking the olive through the window to the square below.

"The doves of peace," Ramona said, and laughed.

***

The Garden House Hotel gives onto the banks of the River Cam in Cambridge, just where the higher level of the river from Grantchester finishes and the water rushes down to the lower level, to the backs, the backs of the colleges. Alistair had insisted on taking out a punt along the river, and Maria had acquiesced. Now Alistair had returned to his books, and Maria was taking tea with Carmen in the hotel, modern Cambridge.

Carmen had placed Maria's business report on the table to her left, and looked at Maria with a liquid gaze of interest and invitation to speak her thoughts, and speak them Maria did, with the full force of the presentation she had rehearsed many times over, just as Carmen would have rehearsed for her performances, just as Carmen rehearsed years ago with Caroline in the cafés of Paris. This was Maria's opportunity, this was her moment and she would take it, as she knew there would be no second chance, not with Carmen.

Maria understood that Carmen's love of music, song, of opera, was not a love of its forms and conventions but a love of the life behind it. In her exposition Maria contrasted the flamenco dancers in the woods with the pomposity of Verdi's marches in Aida; she situated the musical conventions within their times, within the mores of their society and within their society's economic and technical means. She talked of the threads of artistic and cultural development, of the inseparability of the heritage of the past from the present, of continuity of evolution. She hummed melodies to make her points and she struck postures to underline them. What she did was to speak Carmen's language to Carmen, with all the sophistry that Carmen too had learnt, and she channelled all her enthusiasm into the mellifluous development of the proposition. Finally, she knotted all the threads in the present, into her proposal, the same proposal as was bound in black and white in a different language in the report on the table beside Carmen, the language of the advisors.

"Carmen, our film will pulsate with the simplicity and fire of our folk heritage, with the power and sophistication of the classics, our film, the medium of our time," Maria concluded.

"I am to be a film star?" Carmen was a stage performer, not a film star, and knew this.

"You are more than a film star. That is why we will not shoot this as a film. This will be real. We will film our reality, not fragments that we piece together, cut copy and edit. We will have the vibrancy of the real," Maria answered. And what enchanted Carmen was that the young Maria in the film would fuse into her, Carmen, that they would jointly play the main role. As Maria talked of her old style upbringing, Carmen could see how well suited Maria was to play the young roles from the days of her grandmother's tales in Andalusia, and how this would merge into her, Carmen, as the themes were developed through into the present day, and I bag Buenos Aires of the 1930s, she told Maria with a gay laugh. Carmen listened rapturously to Maria who seemed to have the most amazingly detailed plots and descriptions, that Carmen felt she could see the film depicted in Maria's words.

After tea they crossed the river and walked along its banks towards Grantchester, as Carmen spoke of her days in Argentina, a happy time, but one that belonged to her past. They enthused about the young lives they had both lived in Spain, and Maria began to wonder what it was that they were doing in England, but then Maria remembered that Carmen's enthusiasm was essential and to serve her purposes. Is making films not expensive, Carmen had asked her, and Maria had continued undaunted with the flow of her spiel.

Alistair had given Maria an introduction to a lawyer, her subterfuge to make contact with him, and she knew how she would take it from there. In the meantime, she asked Carmen to make sure Alistair read the summary, to make sure she had his support for her role. The thought that Alistair might be invited to finance the film did not for one moment enter Carmen's head.

Maria left Cambridge that evening, and as she drove down the M11, she was obliged once again to ponder the Ramona problem. Her intended source of funds could remain unspoken at present, but somehow she would have to tell Ramona that she, Maria, who had always worked with Ramona on her plots, was about to collaborate on a grand scale with Ramona's mother, with her estranged, recovered, lukewarm mother. Why did I not think this aspect of things through after all the research and effort, and why can I not talk to Ramona, my best friend, about my own major project, she wondered, as she drove, and yet she knew the answer: the project was more important than anything.

Even the most awkward of problems are thrown into perspective by London's traffic system, particularly if you endeavour to cross from the root of the M11 to central London and Knightsbridge: a journey undoubtedly so high on the list of worst journeys of the world, that not even the best collection of CDs can rescue you from its tedium and frustration; and then the interminable search for a residents' parking space. The Maria who stepped through the door of the flat was well on her way to fully paid up membership of the Monster Raving Loony Party, which undoubtedly had a more pragmatic solution to London's traffic problem than had been implemented by any other political party to date, left, right or centre.

For the first time in her life Ramona felt intimidated by Maria, as Maria launched into the description of her project. It seemed to Ramona that she was under threat, not because of a power struggle, but because of a shifting balance that she could not describe, but that left her feeling vulnerable, that old feeling when she just wished to curl up at Clara's feet as Clara read to her on a winter's evening. And Maria? She felt her own violence imposing itself on Ramona and she knew her objective was secure. Her focus could now shift to the advisors, she thought, wondering at her single-mindedness of purpose, and beginning to understand the Carmen who had left her little girl with Clara in the mountains beyond the northern boundary of Andalusia, her little girl Ramona.

CHAPTER TEN

CLUNK

Ramona

Outside term time Alistair worked from his study at home, and this was just such a time. Alistair worked long hours and hard on his studies, but as to gas bills, electricity, water etc. he had tried his damndest, unsuccessfully, to ignore them. As to his business interests, there he had been successful: powers of attorney to his lawyers and accountants had freed him of this troublesome burden.

At seven p.m. he would relax with a glass of sherry in his red-studded leather chair before the fireplace, which he would meticulously lay each morning and flick in a match at 6.30 p.m., his one chore (apart from cooking, which was not a chore for him), his one luxury. Often in these recent months of her presence, Carmen would join him. He would talk of his work and she would listen, and then she would talk of her work, and he would not listen. It was a pleasant convention, he thought, but had never asked what she thought - she came and that was enough for him. It may sound so distant from the romantic encounter at the Anchor, so many years ago, but it was not. Consider that it was less stiff, less exciting, let us say, mature not young.

This evening was not different: it became different. It became different not when Carmen entered the room, but when Alistair opened the letter, and not even then, when he read the letter, and still not even then, quite.

"Carmen, this is unusual." He almost discarded the letter half read, but did not. "Hmm, Mortimer suggests I make a film, sorry, finance a film."

Carmen listened, disinterested but listening, as was her style in these sessions. Unlike Alistair, she would not turn off, hibernate.

"You'll like this," he said. "...it's." He looked up. He looked down and up again. "Carmen...?" He passed the letter to her, and she started to read, she looked up again, and she continued to read, she put the letter down, and for the first time in her life, she was lost for words, Carmen was lost for words. She remembered what she had thought about Ramona and the prize, the book, Cambridge, her suspicions, but now she was lost for words.

"Carmen?"

"I...I know no more than she said to me by the river."

"Carmen? Films?"

"I don't know."

"Do you want this?"

"Yes."

"Then I'll sign."

The magnitude of Alistair's decision struck Carmen, but the poignancy was lost. Even now, after the early years, after knowing she had learnt the way to Alistair's heart, and had always known, she had not learnt that the way to his coffers was much easier than the way to his heart. It eluded her still, and him - the cause of all their problems.

And Alistair was enthused with the subject, the history, the philology, the music, so that for the first time he saw a purpose for his wealth, knowing secretly that this way it may become much more. He would be the lead investor with fifty one percent, and the others would follow. Carmen would be a star and so would Maria. But who was behind it? Carmen had the letter and seemed to know, but she wanted him to sign and he signed. She took the page from him, duly vetted by the lawyers, signed by him, still to be witnessed, and said, "Maria impressed me from that very first of two times that we have met her. I'll just go next door to have Jules witness this, who better than Jules." Alistair was mystified and awaited her return, empty handed as it happens.

"Where's the contract?" he asked.

"In the post," she said. "Why?"

At breakfast the next morning, Alistair returned to the subject.

"I think we should have kept a copy, Carmen."

"Sorry?"

"The contract."

"I think we should have not, Alistair."

"But we do... keep copies."

"Not in this case, Alistair."

"Why ever not?"

"Alistair, your wealth is your curse. You don't want to know."

"But I..."

"Alistair, you did not read the letter. You read the start of the letter. Mortimer was telling you the proposition..."

"So?"

"He was telling you the proposition because he felt obliged to let you know, you know, with me as star and so on, but he advised you not to invest so much in one basket. You did not read that bit." Carmen looked at him benignly.

"So we won't."

"Oh, but you have, Alistair, you have."

"But I..."

"Forget it, Alistair, it's not important. We're having breakfast and then we have work to do, you and I." But suddenly it was important, very important. However, Carmen was able to ensure that however important it may be, it was too late.

***

Maria, twenty-three years old, graduated, musician, best friend of Ramona, ex-Andalusian anachronism, having never shot even a film with a video camera, had become a high budget film producer, beyond a film producer's dreams, within days. Did she rejoice? She did not rejoice. Her single-minded purpose had taken over.

Now, what must I do now, she asked herself. Now I must deal with Ramona in the context of the film (she can be my script writer for the script I write myself) and I must keep Clara out of the picture, yes, I must keep Clara out of the picture. I know I must, even though I do not know why. That is the difficult part, and then the easy part: I must hire casts of thousands, qualified thousands, to make the picture, as I wish it to be made, which is so different from how all the rest of them do it. How do I do that? Technicians, actors, singers, directors, painters, film sets, sound, marketing, presales, make-up, dress, studios...and she continued with the credits at the end of the film and more. I love it. I can do it. I will do it. Basta.

In the house in Cambridge, Carmen was not dreaming of stardom, but rather thought of Maria. Carmen thought of the roles she, Carmen, had played, of the years of training, the memorising, the effort, the power, the instruction, the direction, the make-up, the big day, the health. And that is just me she thought, yet there is a whole film to be made here, not just acted but created, devised, written, recorded, not just recorded, but marketed, not just marketed, but distributed, advertised, and above all, accepted, desired, viewed. She is brave: does she have it? Then she laughed to herself softly: I do not have his money; Ramona does not have his money; Maria has his money. Perhaps Maria can do it.

The Reading Group

"This is dramatic, Ramona," Vera said. "We've had a novel within a novel and now we get a film." Somehow, Vera failed to appreciate the negative side of what she said, but then she was so spontaneous on this occasion, unusually, that it was forgiven.

"For me, as writer, this is the heart of the novel," Ramona replied. "We love reading, but we can do so much more with film. If I cannot do it with film, then at least I can have a film in my novel." She smiled at them, as she often did, inviting response, critical or otherwise.

"I agree," Pam assented eagerly, " I much prefer films." And then she looked down, feeling very stupid, but Ramona rescued her.

"We all prefer films, Pam, because they are fun and novels are work, but I know you love that too. I have seen you in action here, and respect your opinions, as do we all." It was Pam's turn to smile in a mixture of recognition and embarrassment.

"Is Maria a tough nut?" Gloria asked, reaching for the cashews.

"She's so much like Carmen," Vera said, "in her way. Wants to get things done. Loves music. Engages the world, unlike Ramona, sorry Ramona, who sits back a bit."

"This is why I love our group," Ramona lied through her teeth, "You get it all."

"What about Alistair?" Vera asked.

"My man." It was Gloria. "I love Alistair. He's the man. He comes out right." Gloria failed to see the mystification on the faces of the others, and continued, "Alistair is the wronged man, by the females of this novel. Ramona, introduce me."

"Gloria," Ramona admonished, as usual, "let's stick to the text." But Ramona remembered this remark, and she wondered about Gloria, and she wondered about Alistair.

It was time to retire, but the evening had been fun. It was fun to be back with Ramona's book and this part of the book was fun invigorating, learning about Maria, the film. They loved it.

Ramona

It was the lawyer, Mortimer, who had advised Maria of her successful application. He had been astonished and also pleased to be able to give her the good news. He also had to admire her understanding of Alistair's approach. Maria had explained that she had given Alistair a copy of her proposal (which was true but it lay unread in his study), and that she had discussed it at length with Carmen (which was true), and that Alistair's daughter, her flatmate, the literature prize winner, would be the key figure in the project (which was conjecture). Alistair will take to the literary angle, she had told Mortimer, but he will not wish to be burdened by the business aspects.

I am aware that you have full authority to act for Alistair, she had said, and my proposition to you is simple but conditional: you review the proposal and negotiate with me to your entire satisfaction; you then make your recommendation to Alistair if you are positively inclined, or we drop it if you are not; your recommendation to Alistair will be accompanied by a formal acceptance in full for Alistair's signature; you may wish to recommend a lesser scale of involvement (and I think you will), but I insist that Alistair be given an initial opportunity for his 100% buy-in to the idea, and, through his formal acceptance, to ratify what you have negotiated and will sign, such that you are not exposed, and such that I am confident that there will be no back-tracking. She had gone on to explain how this fitted with Alistair's approach, and Mortimer had to agree that she had Alistair to a tee.

And now it had all happened. Carmen had seemed enthusiastic, chivvying Mortimer along (Carmen whom he knew socially but not in business) to get all the formalities done, and the expected call from Alistair, the hesitant have-I-done-the right-thing call, took days to come. Mortimer had glibly confirmed to Alistair that he had carried out Alistair's instructions, albeit at a higher level of investment than he, Mortimer, had recommended and felt that he had covered the risks contractually, but of course the business risk remained. Mortimer had made a clear file note of the conversation, placing it next to Alistair's formal acceptance in the file. It had been Maria's suggestion that the acceptance also include a clause in which Alistair noted and accepted Mortimer's business interests in the deal, and very satisfactory these terms were that Maria had offered him. She enthused with him over the business side, but by the time she left his office in the late afternoon, it was his personal interests in her, he felt, that were more complicated than he expected.

What became clear to Maria very quickly was that she no longer needed to stage a family reunion for Ramona: she could simply call a business meeting, which she would chair.

And in the Sierra Morena, as the heat of the day faded, Clara sat in her corner of the school yard beneath the orange trees, a bottle of Rioja beside her glass, oblivious to developments in the English branch of her family.

CHAPTER ELEVEN

TAKING THE CHAIR

Ramona

"But surely we can't call the film, *Clunk!*" Carmen exclaimed, to nods of agreement from around the table.

"I think it's Maria's little joke," Ramona said, similarly surprised.

And Maria? She wanted to light a fuse to fire up the meeting with a bang and then call it to order, assert control: the name, *Clunk,* was contained in her opening remarks. She had hired a room at the Lanesborough hotel near Hyde Park Corner, neutral territory a short walk from their flat. She had invited Mortimer, Alistair's lawyer, to sit in as an observer, principally to exclude family issues: this was a business meeting, the first. The meeting commenced the moment Alistair and Carmen arrived. Small talk (or large talk), niceties (or nasties) were for later.

Maria sat upright at the head of the long conference table, held up a hand for silence, and looked steadily at each of them in turn, Alistair, Carmen, Ramona and Mortimer, calling the meeting to order with her body language. She was the Speaker on the woolsack in parliament.

"I will answer your question, but first, if you will permit, I will explain how these meetings are conducted. It's simple: I am in the Chair, as I will be at every single one of these meetings I attend, which means that I control the agenda, today my agenda, and we deal exclusively with the agenda. Any questions?" There was mild shock, but no questions.

"Right. There are two parts to my answer on the question of Clunk. If you each look in your provisional contracts you have signed, you will see that I, as producer, can name the film whatever I like, at my sole discretion. That's the first part. Now for Clunk. It's a modern name, neutral, unevocative, onomatopoeic. It is the film that will give power to *Clunk*, the word, just as with your name, Carmen, which is now so closely associated in the minds of many with that role you play so well. What are reservoir dogs? Ask Quentin Tarantino, and he might tell you, no special significance, reservoir dogs are him, Mr Blue, Mr White, Mr Pink etc., and now for millions it means violence and music. I could have been traditional and descriptive or I could have called the film, *Ramona*, but that's old hat, maybe for books but not for us in the vibrant world of film. So you see the answer lies not in what Clunk is but in what Clunk will be."

Even the headstrong audience Maria was addressing took note of her words, understanding the merit of her thoughts, though not settled in their minds on her chosen syllable, but it could wait. Maria continued with her agenda. Her intention was to prepare for the first brainstorming session on the film, on the artistic side, to ensure that each of them was aware of their respective roles, and to establish a management structure for the project, given that she had none of the capabilities of established film studios, or the rest.

Humankind is well able to operate within established structures: a child in class may raise it's hand to speak; an athlete may cross the start line at the sound of the gun; a UN peace keeper, blue-helmeted soldier, may return enemy fire once he is dead, and cannot. It is when these structures break down or do not exist that the problems start, such as ill discipline in class, multiple false starts, or blind shooting of civilians. Would there have been a structure to control the first meeting of Ramona with her parents together? Perhaps, perhaps not, but be that as it may, the meeting for the making of *Clunk* established a structure in which the reunion of the three, Ramona with Carmen and Alistair together, actually took place, an appropriate structure given that the two sides were in reality so independent of one another, if one excludes the fiasco of the book, *A Melody of Sadness*. Significantly, the unborn progeny of Alistair and Carmen, the sister-to-be, could not be a topic in this structure, at least not until the business agenda was finished, by which time a de facto reunion would have occurred.

As an observer, Mortimer had been forbidden to speak (not easy for a lawyer); yet he was grateful of the opportunity to attend. Despite being in his early thirties, athletic, of medium height, traditionally eligible, he was unmarried and did not, in business life, typically encounter the likes of Carmen, Ramona and Maria, the latter two being of more than legal interest. Maria asked him to step outside, while they discussed certain matters. She wanted a lawyer to appoint and control the multitudes of lawyers she would need and sought the advice of the others as to whether he was to be their man. He was.

Maria had arranged a formal three-course lunch to follow the meeting. While the table was being set they moved outside for aperitifs, and Mortimer extracted a camera and tripod from his bag, and endeavoured to extract maximum charm from his persona.

"Ladies, *the first meeting photograph* is my ploy," he said setting up the tripod, "which I will take on the timer, but then Alistair and myself will be excused for a moment while I concentrate on the more aesthetic aspects of photography." And amateur though Mortimer was, that is when the world famous photograph of the producer/director/actress/singer, actress/singer and the prize winning writer was taken, the signed original of which was to fetch the highest price ever for a photograph at auction in New York, and engender years of legal dispute over copyright and ownership, but that was later.

After lunch Mortimer offered a lift, but Ramona and Maria chose to walk home. They crossed into Hyde Park and strolled westwards along Rotten Row, the afternoon sun filtering through the trees, the air alive with the low rumble of airliners bound for Heathrow, none of which they noticed. Maria was thrilled with the results of her first film meeting, and her enthusiasm had been shared by them all.

"I should be jealous," Ramona said, "I thought you were my best friend, but you and Carmen, wow. We couldn't stop you over lunch."

"She's got it, she's a performer, Ramona, and like me she vibrates to *Clunk*, as much of the world soon will, I hope." For a moment neither of them could control their laughter.

Ramona broke off first and spoke. "You've really caught me, too, today, and I do like Mortimer, with your vision. It's just great, but you know, I'm not sure how you do it, get it on canvas, like a painting. How do you paint a dream? I can't."

"First you spend a hundred million dollars, and then you worry about it. That's what the others do." Maria did not want to get into the subject at this point, to feed her own concerns on just that subject. It was daunting, to be taken a step at a time.

"You didn't congratulate them on the baby." Maria broke the pause.

"I think you do that when it's born, Maria."

"Agree to be godmother."

"You've agreed for me already, Maria."

"Well, I'm going to be one too, Ramona. God, I hope this doesn't screw up the film preparations."

"Come, come, Maria, knowing Carmen's history as you do?" They walked on in silence through the noise of the park.

Mortimer returned to his office in Belgravia, mulling over the course things were taking. He resolved to devote substantial time to this film venture. If it worked, it would be fantastic for him with the terms Maria had given him, a new league, and then, well, Maria and Ramona, but maybe Ramona was a touch cool for him.

For his part, as they headed ponderously along the arterially clogged A11, Alistair determined that he too would put effort into the film, contributing his literary and critical skills. Carmen smiled as he told her this, wondering with her right hemisphere whether Maria would attribute the same value to his professorial talents as he did, while her left hemisphere hummed with the prospect of film stardom. She pressed the button for CD number four, and the descendants of musicians, roughly six generations down the line, picked up where Beethoven's pen had scrawled his ninth symphony, giving her for a second a glimpse of *Clunk* in a Clockwork Orange. If only Beethoven knew, she thought, but then he was deaf, wasn't he?

"Is *Clunk* to you what it is to me?" Alistair asked, and Carmen realised that he had asked the best question of the day - perhaps he did have a contribution to make.

The Reading Group
Ramona reached for her water glass and gave the group an enquiring glance.

"I haven't heard of the film, *Clunk,*" Gloria said.

"Stick with the text, Gloria. It's not made yet, is it?" Gloria's familiar pattern, Ramona thought.

"Clunk, clunk," Pam said. "Can I choose the title? I mean not Clunk."

"Pam, you're following Gloria now into the real world. Shall we keep to the literary sphere?" Ramona struck a long-suffering pose.

"I think I'll make tea," Vera said, and Ramona began to feel that the whole purpose of the group was breaking down in a way she had not anticipated. For moments such as this, she had a bottle of Carlos theThird (Tercero) Spanish brandy in her bag, appropriate to the book and to the stimulation of the literary process, and not yet used.

"Forget the tea, Vera. Let's inject some local colour," Ramona said, pulling out the bottle with a flourish. "Just some glasses, Vera, thanks."

"This is why they knock back the port after dinner at high table in Cambridge," Pam said. "In service of the humanities and the sciences."

"Let's give it a try then," Gloria suggested, perking up. "You know I finally read that Norwegian book, you know, the one where the character turns into a fiction, doesn't really exist, bit like getting sucked into cartoon world really."

"Let's drink to our staying out of cartoon world, Gloria," Ramona proposed, "but let me warn you, Gloria: you try stepping one more time out of my novel, *Ramona,* into the real world, and I'll write a sequel in which I stick you fair and square in cartoon world. Agreed?"

"You've made your point Ramona. I'll respect your privacy. Cheers."

The bottle circulated a second time, despite grimaces and gasps at its strength - it is true that it was authentically illicit - and the spirit picked up.

"There is no question that it is problematic," Vera stated, "to have you in our group and to read *Ramona,* for obvious reasons, so I think we should talk about it, clear the air."

"It's OK for me," Ramona replied. "I think we just have to separate the person Ramona, me, and book *Ramona,* the novel."

"Isn't that a bit like Nazi prison guards only taking orders?" Pam contributed.

"I don't see the connection," Ramona said.

"I mean, it's like, you know, we're not mechanical, we know

what we're doing." Pam answered, and Ramona wondered how Pam could know what she was doing if she couldn't even think straight.

"I think Pam means we have feelings about the characters in the book and then one of them is right here," Vera suggested. If that's what Pam means, why didn't Pam say it, Ramona thought, but she said, "We don't delve into the feelings of the writers in this reading group, so why worry about the characters, in as far as they exist outside the book?"

The downward spiral of the discussion continued, paved as it was with good intentions, in the direction of hell. By the time they broke up half an hour later, Ramona was seriously wondering where these people got their education, if any, and from where they had drawn the preposterous notion of their literary pretensions. At least I've won a prize and sold books to prove my credentials, she thought, but she had started reading *Ramona* and she would finish. After *Ramona* she doubted they would want her back.

Gloria offered Ramona a lift home, intending to confront her outside the group, but Ramona had her own vehicle outside, which Gloria noted was a top of the range BMW like her ex-husband drove. She would get even with him one day. The speed with which Ramona shot off would have spun her wheels, if she had not had traction control. She flicked the CD onto a Wagner piece - the modern equivalent of which would be an ultra-violence computer game - and moved through the London evening at points building speed, in god mode.

Ramona

Back in the flat Ramona and Maria relaxed over a bottle of Rioja, while they chatted with Clara on the speakerphone - and not a word on the film, Maria said, unknowingly pre-empting Ramona by a whisker. From the radio in the background floated the deep tones of an old song about a rambling rose and in the foreground the clear Spanish tones of Clara came from the phone, as she told them of Fernando's fiftieth birthday party in Seville, of the cousins, of the school, of home.

As she spoke, Clara visualised the two girls who had shared her home and her schoolyard, and not the Ramona and Maria, the two young ladies, sitting in Knightsbridge. But that was not the real world: the real world is that her larynx was linked to their eardrums, and vice versa, by compressions of air in her house and their flat respectively, connected with alternate streams of electrons and photons. That is the real world, the real world as we understand it.

CHAPTER TWELVE

BOHEMIOS

Ramona
If we do not know whether light travels in waves or as particles, how can
we believe what we see? If I set a four-bladed fan at sixty revolutions per
minute and shine a strobe light on it with sixty pulses per minute the fan
stops for me, and if I quadruple the pulse frequency, it stops again for me.
How can we believe what we see?

If we know of the Doppler effect, how can we believe what we hear?
How do we know we are here, to know what we see and hear...

Alistair looked up from the text of the student's essay he was
marking as Carmen came in.

"This is complete and utter crap. This kid's writing about *A Tale
of Two Cities* and talking about strobe lights. We've got to change our
admissions procedures."

Carmen glanced at the essay.

"That's Nigel's writing, Alistair. You gave him a "first" for part one
of the tripos."

"So I did. OK, maybe I should read on."

Carmen glanced at the essay's opening words.

"He's just setting you up with scientific claptrap, Alistair. He's
going to talk about fact, fiction and coincidence, artistic licence, and
then he'll ask, why bother about the representational world in that
case, let's all be as absurd as Ionesco, and then he'll come back to say
Kant was right after all, that we don't need to know about noumena,
which we can't anyway, so we might as well live in the phenomenal
world captured and altered by the constructs of our mind, which

projects upon phenomena to perceive them, and then we can continue to view the world through rose-tinted spectacles, which is, of course, what Dickens does not do. Am I right?"

"Carmen, if essays were marked by weight, by number of words, rather than by intelligent content, I think you'd be qualified to give tuition."

"Read the essay. Tell me if I'm right." Carmen struck an arrogant pose.

"What makes you so sure?"

"Nothing. Nothing other than the fact that I had this discussion with Nigel last week. I want him to work on the film. We were talking about folk tales, myth and how the imagination creates them," Carmen waved his interruption aside, "but they have a real world meaning, and I think that is part of the theme of the film. Generally speaking, things that really happened (or warnings of what might happen) are translated into and preserved in myth and folk lore, because it's more fun and easier to remember, like verse." Carmen stopped.

"The film, the film, so it's dominating us all," Alistair said. "It's time for drinks."

But drinks had to wait. The phone rang, Maria for Carmen.

"I just wanted to check with you, Carmen. We'll use Bombay."

"Explain," Carmen suggested.

"Bollywood. Why pay the Americans when we can do it all in India, the film capital of the world, in volume? The point is you'll have to film there." Maria stated.

"Maria, given the choice, I take Bollywood over Hollywood, or Ealing." Maria hung up, and Carmen wondered whether they still made films in Ealing, and then she thought about the last time she had seen a film, and realised that she had seen snatches on television, but herself had never been inside a cinema. They didn't have one where she grew up, and since then, well...

"Alistair," she said, "let's go to the cinema."

"Carmen, you're joking, surely. What do you want to see?"

"Alistair, we're about to make a film." And the same thought dawned on Alistair.

They drove into Cambridge and saw *Desperados*. Carmen loved it:

the Mexican boots, the Hispanic bars, the guitars, and the beautiful heroine.

"This is as good as Carmen," she whispered to Alistair's astonishment, as he watched drug dealers massacred, blood mopped up in bars strewn with gunned down victims, well, mayhem." Again he wondered whether they would all be working on the same film. What was *Clunk?*

***

Mortimer's office was situated on the first floor of a grand Belgravia terrace overlooking gardens. Mortimer's property occupied two houses in the terrace. In the basement was a swimming pool across both houses, the upper section of the one house being rented out by Mortimer, who lived on the ground floor, while the other house was entirely office space, of which his practice took two floors. The reason Alistair was Mortimer's client was the connection of inherited wealth, albeit less in Mortimer's case.

You cannot cause a sensation walking into a Belgravia-housed solicitors office, as that is where the smart people work anyway, unless, of course, you happen to be Ramona and Maria, who could put even the advertising scene to shame. Mortimer's staff were used to his clients, even to his girlfriends, as he lived next door, but let us just say that Mortimer's *milieu* was more staid. They were ushered into his office and settled themselves on the royal blue velvet sofa, sinking deeply.

"Do you have conference table?" Ramona asked from her awkward position sunk in a blue sea of velvet, and they moved through to Mortimer's conference room, mahogany table, traditional dining chairs, could be Spain. Ramona felt much more comfortable.

"Don't you think this is a beautiful office, Ramona," Maria said, and Mortimer beamed, trying unsuccessfully to be business-like.

"We are partners, Mortimer," Maria said, "Ramona and I have been partners for years, and now we have you."

"Well, I..."

"Mortimer, what I am saying is that we work together, no pretence, no secrets. We know you're a lawyer and know a lot, which we don't, so we want you to help us. You saw my questions."

Mortimer relaxed, and went on to answer her questions.

"Maria, Ramona, you have two approaches at either end of the scale and infinite gradations between."

"Tell us."

"In theory you could build a brand new design of supersonic jet airliner over the Internet, contracting out everything: the management, the planning, the design, the manufacturing the marketing..."

"And in practice?" Ramona interrupted.

"You couldn't," he said.

"Tell us what else we can't do," Maria suggested.

"What you also can't do, at least not in a reasonable time frame," he replied, "is the other end of the scale, everything."

"See, I told you, Ramona," Maria exclaimed, "Bollywood." They both laughed and Mortimer looked mystified.

"Mortimer," Ramona was pleased to educate him, "Maria thinks we should shoot the film in India and Andalusia. She thinks we can use their skills, instead of getting involved with the hype of Hollywood. We don't need hype, because we believe in what we are doing, so it will sell."

"I see," he said, not sure that he saw, but needing time to reflect.

"She thinks," Ramona continued, " and I agree, for me, that Hollywood is the more foreign place for us; you see we both had a simple upbringing in the hills of southern Spain."

Mortimer's mind wandered, as he thought about moving his office to southern Spain, the hills, before the reality of his professional situation drew him back to the conference room.

"Do you know anything about this?" he asked.

"No," they answered in unison, and in future years Mortimer would reflect back that this was the moment when he realised that the film would be a stunning success.

The Reading Group

It was Vera who interrupted this time.

"Ramona, this book has moved on from love, Alistair and Carmen, to a business text book."

"Many romances start in the office, Vera," Ramona countered.

"You're being prosaic," Vera responded.

"Love does not choose its location, Vera. Where did the industrial poor on eighteen hour shifts find love two centuries ago?"

"Yes, but..."

"No *but*, Vera. Gloria?" Ramona asked.

"I met my ex-husband at work, the bastard."

"But you loved him then," Ramona pressed.

With a huge amount of willpower Gloria admitted it, "Yes. He ran off with the secretary."

"Snap," Pam said.

"What?" Gloria felt herself to be the butt of a joke.

"She, the secretary, met him in the office too," Pam said, and Gloria turned bright red. Ramona, who had felt Gloria's antagonism realised she was not unique, and Pam had deliberately hit a sensitive spot: her turn to twist the knife.

"Was she his secretary when you met him, Gloria?" Ramona asked sweetly; but she had underestimated Gloria and her uninhibited blunt manner, even in a literary group.

"I was the better you know what, Ramona, but there's more to life. That's what I learnt, and dumped him." Ramona decided not to ask for references, and Vera busied herself with the errant fastening of her left shoe, while Pam's expression displayed that she was perhaps not the dumb Sloane she projected herself to be. I guess she did get into Cambridge after all, Ramona thought. For the first time the reading group was cohesive. I wonder if I could write a novel about a reading group, Ramona asked herself: how what they read influences their relationships; how the group develops (their characters, tensions), falls apart, I wonder, I don't know, what would they read? The idea faded as fast as it formed.

Ramona continued to read.

Ramona

"Bombay would be very felicitous," Mortimer said.

"Why?" Ramona asked.

"Gipsies," he replied.

"*Gitanos, Bohemios,* and?" Maria asked.

"The English word *gipsy* comes from *Egyptian*, where the English thought they came from. Similarly the French say *gitanes,* for them it meant Spanish. But in fact, linguistic scholars discovered much later that the gipsy language, Romany, derives from Hindi. They came from India, north, left-hand side."

"So why's that, what did you say, felicitous?" Ramona asked.

"Flamenco. It's gipsy. So you're filming where they came from, in Bollywood, almost, just a few hundred years out of date and miles south," Mortimer answered.

"You've given me a thought, Mortimer," Maria said. "I've always thought of flamenco as Spanish, kind of mixed up Andalusia, the Moors earlier, and so on. Now, we were going back a couple of hundred years to start the film, but what if we go back another hundred years or so, start with the violent scenes, I guess there would have been some, that drove them out of India. I see them struggling thorough sandy wastes, then across the lush plains of the Indus, travelling at night to avoid the persecution of the Mogul rulers, up into the mountains of Afghanistan harried by the tribes, before crossing into their first refuge of Iran."

"Maria!" Ramona exclaimed, "Have you been studying this?"

"Of course not, but how else would it have happened. Iran's on the way." Maria was enjoying her new role as producer.

"You see you can do more," Mortimer said. "You need to research the cultural heritage. Go to Romania, where there are whole clans of gipsies, very traditional. Get a connection with flamenco, look at the language, the songs, and then go and look for something in India."

"We're not the National Geographic," Ramona protested, envisioning the documentary.

"No, Ramona, he's right." Maria wanted to build on this idea. "We don't document it: we take out fragments and fit them into the mosaic. *Clunk* is, among other things, a mosaic. I might get those Bollywood all-singing-and-dancing tragic heroes and heroines, persecuted lovers, to learn flamenco, glorious." The more she thought about it, the more she thought that there was a more than coinciden-tal similarity to flamenco, but then it was not so long really. If the Moguls kicked out a few gipsies, then you're talking about an even shorter time ago, just a few hundred years, than the troubadours in France, so surely you would expect similarity, you would expect traditions to live, particularly musical ones. The guitars came to flamenco only later.

As if reading her mind, Mortimer said, "Don't forget that the ice cream vans here still play *Greensleeves.*"

"Mortimer, I think we'll go on holiday," Ramona proposed, "to Romania."

"We'll leave next week," Maria added.

Mortimer couldn't believe the invitation: he was bowled over.

CHAPTER THIRTEEN

MORTIMER

Ramona

When you look into a bright light you are dazzled and do not see the surroundings. I, Mortimer, was dazzled by the bright light of Maria, I admit, but during the Romania trip, I will not say it was an eclipse of the sun, Maria still shone bright, but Ramona began to come into focus for me, to emerge quietly, Ramona.

For three years I have worked for Alistair, inheriting his account from my father who inherited Alistair's family's account from his father. Carmen, this wondrous reappearing creature, was a surprise, and then suddenly there was a Carmen of my generation, in the form of Maria, the film producer. I admit that at the time I did believe she was a film producer. I suppose I just assumed it, when she came with the proposal, and so never thought to ask. You may ask whether I was diligent in my examination of the proposal and her credentials. The answer is yes: everything was conditional; Maria had to deliver.

You may ask whether, with the trip to Romania, I was getting too close to my clients for professional comfort, and there the answer is no: I am not a gynaecologist. And if you want to know more, well, a gentleman does not talk - you will hear nothing from me.

We took off from Gatwick at ten and arrived in Bucharest soon after three as a result of the two-hour time difference. As you enter Bucharest you drive through broad tree-lined avenues, but a lot of buildings seem to have had their construction abandoned incomplete, and you cannot miss the centrepiece, the Ceausescu palace, a modern palace. Are the world's greatest men the world's most evil? Certainly Ceausescu will survive in posterity, having drained his country's economy for his monument in the same way as Cathedral construction drained wealth for centuries from medieval Europe. He wanted the largest building in the world, but overlooked the Pentagon. Bad luck, Ceausescu, but you're dead now - it's too late.

We visited the palace on the very first day, a private tour arranged by Ramona's uncle in Spain. Our guide explained the conundrum that faced the Romanian people on the dictator's demise: spend the money to complete the white elephant or suffer an incomplete wasting asset, and they chose the first, to use it for the National Assembly and for international conferences - work continued, for years. Ramona said she preferred the Alhambra, but I have not seen the Alhambra, and in my wildest dreams I could not have imagined the scale of things inside that building in Bucharest, rooms that could house football fields, hand-knotted carpets weighing tons, chandeliers, and marble, marble, marble, floors walls, sculpted, chiselled, and of course, escape tunnels, reflecting the dictator's knowledge of the devotion of his subjects. For a moment, but only a brief one, my attention was diverted from my companions as I marvelled at the palace.

On day two we drove out of Bucharest. The roads reminded me of France, straight and lined with trees. Our driver told us that Romania maintains close cultural links with France, and that their language is a romance language rooted in Latin. But the road was rough and the further we drove from Bucharest, the more agricultural it became. Horses pulled carts laden with hay and straw, as Korean cars wove their way between at crazy speeds, and east bloc vehicles spluttered, occasionally dying by the roadside. As we neared our destination, the houses had strange turrets or towers with a touch of the Pagoda to them. The turrets reflect your status among the gipsy clans, the driver told us; he did not think they had any functional purpose, but the bigger the tower, the better. And then across fields from centuries before would rise gigantic, soviet-style industrial premises, puffing, belching, and no doubt drenching their surrounds in chemical waste.

I did not join the girls in the meetings with the gipsy, as they preferred it to be small and informal, but I did hear music and song floating across the courtyard, as I returned with the driver three hours later. In fact, I was not quite sure why I should be in Romania with the two ladies. Could this really be true?

***

The Reading Group

"That's just what I was wondering," Gloria cut in. "Why on earth did they take Mortimer with them?"

"It does seem a bit forward," Vera added. "They do hardly know him, and it's just a trip to... well, sort of exploratory, isn't it?"

"Let's get to the questions at the end of the session," Ramona suggested, and took up reading where she had left off, at the next section, demarked by asterisks.

Ramona

As they walked through Sloane Square, Ramona remarked to Maria how small it seemed compared to the grand architecture in the heart of Bucharest, and how grey is the sky, Maria responded. They realised that they had wandered down too far south and were making a detour. It would take them about twenty minutes to walk from their flat to Mortimer's office, their second visit. Mortimer's secretary showed them into his office, advising them that he was stuck in a taxi on his way back from the City and would be another fifteen minutes. She brought them tea and they sank into the blue velvet sofa.

"Hellish uncomfortable, and immodest," Maria said, struggling to her feet. She moved across to the chair at Mortimer's desk and assumed the role of solicitor, shuffling papers.

"A diary." Maria waved a slim brown leather book in the air.

"It might be personal, Maria."

"That is *why* I shall read it," Maria laughed, and Ramona shrugged her shoulders, raised her eyebrows, sipped her tea, until Maria's laughter echoed through the office. She came back to the blue velvet sofa and sank down next to Ramona.

"I think we should read it together." And they started to read, Maria casting an enquiring eye before flipping to the next page, and the next for several minutes. As they reached the end, they looked at one another in amused astonishment.

"Hard to believe but true," Maria said. "He's fantasising that he came on the trip to Romania with us."

"The secret life of Mortimer. Quite clever the way he manages to flatter both of us at once." They laughed, but Ramona was asking herself if perhaps Mortimer were sending her a secret message, if *that* was the secret. Why was he late and why was the diary lying exposed on his desk? And it was rather charming, *a gentleman doesn't talk:* charming, innuendo, or invitation?

They stood to greet Mortimer as he came in, smiling at them graciously. As he shook Maria's hand he took the diary from her and dropped it on the corner of the desk.

"Let's go through to the conference room," he said. "I'm longing to hear about Romania."

They took their places at the mahogany table, not with embarrassment but with amusement, although neither Ramona nor Maria quite knew how to start, so it was Mortimer who broke the silence.

"You liked my little joke?" He smiled at them.

"Well," Ramona began.

"No, no, let me explain," Mortimer interrupted. "When we met here last week, I did think you had asked me to join you, and then you were gone. Anyway, is that what Bucharest is like, the way I wrote it?"

Maria thought back to the conversation here last week, looked at Ramona.

"You know, come to think of it, I think Ramona did kind of invite you, but I organised the trip, and it didn't occur to me. Sorry, Mortimer, next time. I guess that's what you're angling at."

"I like your writing style, Mortimer," Ramona added. "It's a bit like mine. I also like your unconventional manner of making the point, with the *diary.* I suppose we should be embarrassed at reading, unasked, your personal papers, diary."

"What else would I have expected?" Mortimer was pleased with his little ploy.

"Next time, though, I want the unexpurgated version," Maria said, "I want the sex scenes, but I demand the right to edit them first, if only for verisimilitude."

"They're locked in the desk, Maria," Mortimer quipped. "I've lost the key. Sorry. But as you said. Next time. You know where I am."

"Can you handle us both?" Ramona silkily enquired, unconsciously asking him to make his choice, but Mortimer was a lawyer and left the contract open-ended.

Maria briefly described the meeting with the gipsies in Romania. She thought that it was going to be easier than they supposed to research the subject. Although they were scattered all over the world, she told him, they had very cohesive communities, *and* - this was the point - there was a movement to link up worldwide under the name they liked to use now, "Rom", so Maria felt that a lot would have already been done for them and should be easily accessible, if they could make the right connections.

And then there was Alistair. He should be able to point them in the right direction for linguistic research. This was critical, she had been told, to track back how the gipsies had spread geographically through common words incorporated or lost in the languages of the different geographical communities. It's truly fascinating how much you can work out from those key words, and to demonstrate it, Maria proved her conjecture last week about Iran: namely, all the language varieties were peppered with Farsi, the language of Iran.

But it was the music and the dance that struck us most, Ramona told Mortimer, the power, the familiarity, the intermingling of the complex and the simple. Both Maria and Ramona believed that they had a powerful foundation for *Clunk*, a source of free material, and a whole dimension of enchantment to add to the flamenco theme.

"You know," Maria said, "If it weren't the case that I have to spend Alistair's cash, I'd seriously think about doing a low budget film, using material and people from the real world. But I guess I've signed the contract, so I'll spend the money just like it says."

As they rose to leave, Ramona suggested Mortimer come round for drinks after work, to make amends. He agreed.

Many men are gullible enough to believe they chose the woman in their life: few women believe this to be the case, fewer even than the number who believe they chose the right man. These were Maria's cynical thoughts as they walked back, this time taking the shorter route along Chesham Place, into Pont Street and across Sloane Street. Ramona had found a house she was interested to buy in Hans Place, just behind Harrods, and wanted to take another look from the outside, but she was in two minds, reluctant to move away from their flat so close to the park. Should I leave the field clear for Ramona? Maria wondered to herself, as they walked. Do I have a choice? What does *he* want? Does he know? Clearly something is going on, but I am not sure what. Should I ask Ramona? She's looking very coy. What does *she* want? Does she know?

The Reading Group

For the first time, they were meeting at Gloria's, on a beautiful day outside in her small but charming garden. It was incredible to think that Kensington High Street, the noise and bustle of London, was just two hundred yards away behind the buildings - only the occasional siren breached that mass. Here you could hear birds sing in the foliage of the trees above, and on days like this sit in the gentle breeze, imagining yourself in Clara's schoolyard.

"I think I do owe Ramona an apology," Gloria said.

"Fire away, Gloria," Ramona responded.

"You know, the plot. I thought it was all getting a bit out of hand, when we just had the first bit. But now, well it kind of does fit together. It's the earlier time in Spain that brings them together in the frame. Gets Maria in the picture." Gloria had got it out.

"I think so too," Vera said. "I went back to the prologue, and it's just that we, the reader, are shown what was supposed to be the story. What was recorded?"

"What the world believed," Pam added, "and would never have known otherwise, if Carmen had not read the press clipping on the prize."

"But who sent her the press clipping?" Ramona asked, and seeing their consternation, added, "Just a question. No hidden intent. Don't worry."

"I suppose," Vera stated thoughtfully, "whoever did send it could have prompted Carmen in some other way."

"I agree. Worth bearing in mind," Ramona suggested.

"What I think is quite good too," Vera started a new topic, "is the way we see Carmen the seventeen-year-old and now we see the mature Carmen, same person but in a different world."

"That's what it's like," Pam agreed. "Teenagers do live in a different world. I'm a bit older than you, but I know my twenties, post Cambridge, were nothing like my teens."

"And then we have Maria and Ramona," Ramona said. "And

isn't it true, that they live in a different world, like we do, because our world now is different to Alistair's Cambridge of the seventies. Well, I guess. I wasn't even born then, well, in a manner of speaking."

Once again, Ramona felt the discussion was going nowhere, and picked up the book to continue.

Ramona

Back at the flat Maria sat at her desk reflectively. She flipped open her laptop, and once it had completed its routine clicking and chattering, went online to check her email - the machine would check automatically for her later at one o'clock, but she would take a look now anyway. Nothing new and the machine disconnected. She clicked on *New,* and the email template filled the screen. She tapped in *Mort,* and the name Mortimer leapt into the recipient box. She began to type.

> To... Mortimer
> Cc... Ramona
> Subject: Gentlemen do not Talk?

The restaurant served the most extraordinary fish dishes, supplied I suppose by the Danube, and then we returned to the hotel, retiring after a drink at the bar. A fascinating day, an exciting country and then, of course, my companions.

I must have been dozing when I heard a light knock on the door. I rolled out of bed, slipped on the hotel's white terry towel bathrobe and went to the door. Hardly had I released the catch, than it opened a few centimetres and Maria slipped through. She wore a deep red garment cut low and very, very short. She linked her arms around my neck and pulled me towards her. The door clicked shut behind her. Her hands dropped to give a deft tug on the belt of my robe, which parted and I felt her fingers walking slowly towards the small of my back. I clasped her hips, pulling her towards me, her garment slid up gently and I felt her guide me home. She sank into my embrace and I eased us down to the floor, where she came alive to her passion. Rolling, she was above me, her lustrous dark hair hanging down around that expression of fire glittering in her eyes, and then we were rolling again, and she was arching into me ... but gentlemen do not talk.

I did not realise she had left, but dawn was breaking outside, when I awoke to hear her knock on her return in the early morning. This time I ignored the bathrobe and with a mix of sleep and desire crossed to the door. I swung open the door. It was Ramona! She looked at me standing framed naked in the doorway, smiled, pushing me back as she stepped inside, dressed in a shimmering full-length cream nightgown. My mind told me this was complicated, I did not want this, but my physicality belied this, evident as it was to Ramona, who took my hand and led me to the bed. I reached up to her shoulders and the nightgown simply fell away to nothing in a circle on the floor around her feet. She stroked my chest with her hands and gently pushed my back on the bed, gently, languishingly, gently it went on for ever and ... but gentlemen do not talk. At breakfast the next morning...

Maria printed out a copy of the email draft, dropped it on the coffee table and went to her bedroom.

It did not take long.

"Maria!" came as a shriek from, presumably, the coffee table. Maria went through to Ramona.

"You haven't sent this!" Ramona exclaimed.

"Why not? He's got to know the choice," Ramona responded, "I mean, how else will he find out."

"Maria." That warning tone.

"OK, I didn't send it, but it's very funny. I think it's funny." Maria may have thought it funny, but Ramona was not sure what to think. She exacted Maria's commitment to deletion, destruction.

Maria returned to her desk and the laptop. Adding a sense of the risqué to the sense of fun, she hit the *send* button, knowing full well the email would go into her outbox where she could delete it before going back online. She was interrupted by the phone ringing in the entrance hall, and answered to the electrician checking if he could come by after one. After one, she looked at her watch, my god, she dropped the phone and raced to the laptop to see *Two of two tasks completed successfully* as the machine disconnected after the automatic one o'clock session - the email had not only left but also, no doubt, arrived. At least I had better delete Ramona's copy, Maria thought, as she logged on to Ramona's account. Maybe I can keep this between me and Mortimer.

Twice a day Mortimer's secretary would categorize his incoming emails and print them for him, at nine in the morning and at three in the afternoon. At three thirty she came upon *Gentlemen do not talk?* Wow, she thought as she read it, visualising the two girls. Must be something to do with the film. Or? With a frisson of jealousy, she did not print this one out, but positioned the cursor on it and dragged the electronic file into a folder, only accessible as all her folders with her secret password, a folder named *Blackmail.* An incipient email correspondence between Maria and Mortimer had been dealt an untimely fate.

Mortimer looked at the email files his secretary had brought in. He had a colour coding system: the red file was what his secretary determined to be high priority; the green file contained items she had dealt with herself, just to let him know; and they had named the third file blue as in cold, because it contained items of such urgency that they could wait until hell froze over. A year ago Mortimer had suggested a new category for junk mail, jokes etc., where it was not worth wasting the paper to print them. What shall I do with them, she had asked, and he simply told her to burn them. Knowing the rules on document retention, and naturally cautious, she had quipped, burnt, carbon copies then, OK, we've got red, green and blue, the *Blackmail* folder. Mortimer had long since chosen to rely on his secretary and ignore the *Blackmail.*

The Reading Group
Pam could not contain her laughter.

"Sorry, Ramona, but that is just so corny, the red, the green, the blue and the blackmail."

"And then we thought we had a juicy scandal," Vera cut in, "a nice juicy blackmailing and it turns out you're talking about the trash can."

"She leads us along and then she drops us," Gloria said, feeling miffed with this coming so soon after her apology to Ramona. "This is what she keeps doing, like we had a kidnapping at the beginning which turns out to be the kid going to stay with it's auntie, well more or less." She paused and then continued, as the heat built within her. "We can be more brutal. Don't you think there's a danger the book might become a bit trivial, I mean if everything is always brought down a peg, blackmail to the trash can as Vera put it?"

Ramona observed as the discussion continued between

them, thinking back to their changing positions as the plot unfolded. If only they could wait, she thought, hold back with their premature views, but they can't.

CHAPTER FOURTEEN

KARMA, FATE, INCARNATION

Ramona

"The way I see it, you want to create your own artistic reality in the film, not a scientific truth," Alistair opined.

Maria sat next to him in the punt, as Carmen, standing on the stern, expertly manoeuvred them along the backs. To the left, in the distance you could see the tower of Cambridge University library and to the right King's college, its palatial edifice beside the chapel with green lawns fronting the river, another Cambridge blue day with a slight nip in the air.

"If we engage some academic type," he continued, "you'll find he has specialised in some abstruse aspect of language, customs or whatever. Everything *we* need to know is published."

Carmen stowed the pole and sat down opposite them.

"I love your idea of starting with a haunting Indian refrain. I can see plains beside the river, hills behind, a melody floating towards us as the camera closes in on two lovers, lagging behind an itinerant group heading westwards, as the sun gently sinks behind the hills silhouetted against the reddening, darkening sky." Carmen raised her arms and let out the final notes of an unknown song.

"We shall call her Karmi and him Romi," Maria suggested, with a laugh. "Karmi, like Karma, your Karma, your incarnation, your lot in life, your fate, or like Carmen where fate is taking us, the Carmen of flamenco, our Karma. Romi, like Rom, gipsy, Romany. Fated to love, sing and suffer, we shall resurrect them in successive generations."

"Perhaps he should not be Rom but Yahya, not a gipsy." The water rippled around Carmen's fingers. "I see him marching through the highlands of Yemen to the sound of flutes and the polyrhythmic beat of drums, crossing the immense sandy wastes of Arabia. It is he who brings the Arabic, the Moorish to flamenco, when after years of adventure he arrives in Andalusia, and steals Karmi from her family, hides her in the valleys of the Sierra Nevada, suffers the winter snows and the summer heat."

Alistair: "Weren't the Moors more Morocco, Algeria, Mauritania?"

"We are creating our own artistic reality, Alistair. I prefer Yemen today, the Arabian Peninsula, dhows trading along the coast, Ali Babar, Sinbad," Carmen responded.

Maria: "Yahya marches through the highlands with his band of men to the sound of flutes and the polyrhythmic beat of drums, followed by the caravan of camels, women and children, the survivors of a bloody massacre in the nomadic north, a massacre in which he lost his father; Yahya is now leader, and he lost his betrothed. They descend to the lowlands, to the port. Heavy of heart, he watches the men unload the camels and stow their trading goods on dhows; he watches the dhows cast their lines; hardly a breath of wind, he watches the dhows drift, their Lateen rigs angled to the sky."

"In that moment grief is tempered by adventure. He throws his purse of gold coins to his men and strides into the sea, soon swimming out to the lead dhow, the last time he is ever seen. After months of adventure on the Arabian coast the dhow reaches the coast of India. He hears tell of the wondrous snow clad mountains to the north - he has never seen snow. Before he reaches those mountains that beckoned him, he encounters the remnants of a tribe fleeing the conquerors of their lands. He falls in love with the chieftain's daughter Karmi, and leads them to safety, as he searches for an overland route westwards towards his home." Maria fell silent and the punt drifted gently with the current. Alistair stood, moved to the stern and took the pole. Carmen was thoughtful. How was she to explain to Maria that she was missing the point? She did not need to.

"Your version's better," Maria said. "It brings us somewhere. I mean links the traditions, while I just added a bit to the beginning of the story. But I think what I'm trying to say is let's get in some of these tremendous landscape scenes, like I described in India, and match them to the music. So now we've got a musical, ethnic and visual weave. Let's not go overboard on the gipsy bit. That just gives us a start in India. It's more the traditions we want than the ethnicity. Let's treat flamenco as a mixed marriage of traditions. That's more of a reality than a factual progression would be. Alistair's right."

"Long live *Clunk!*" Alistair proposed.

"*Clunk* Zindabad!" Carmen added.

The tintinnabulation of Maria's soft laugh rippled the smooth green surface of the river, or perhaps it was the motion of the punt.

Back at the Garden House Hotel, Mortimer was waiting for them, standing outside in the midmorning sun. Maria wanted to talk to them about a trip to India, and she had hoped Ramona would be there, but Ramona had promised to visit Clara for a few days in Spain, and did not wish to cancel that. As they sat over coffee, Maria felt uncomfortable under Mortimer's gaze. Was he thinking of the email, *Gentlemen do not Talk?*, she wondered. Why had he not mentioned it? She wanted to but could not: what should she say? In fact, I'm the one who's thinking about the email, she told herself, not him - maybe he's embarrassed. And he was in a sense embarrassed, not by the email that he had not read, but by Maria's almost furtive behaviour, so he took the easy way out and concentrated on Carmen, while Alistair lost himself in daydreams. But there is only so long, or rather so short a time, that you can ignore Maria, Mortimer found - little more than the time a ball bearing can resist a magnet.

***

Clara met Ramona at Seville airport and in the time-honoured routine set by the little green Seat they ascended into the hills of the Sierra Morena. Bliss to be out of London and in the country, in the sun, with the sound of Spanish, Ramona thought, as they wound their way past rock-strewn slopes. She suggested they stop and walk for a while in the woods higher up. They strolled along the hillside terrace of a plantation in the pine-scented air, and for the moment even the heat did not matter among the shady trees.

"You can read to me tonight from my new book, *Ramona*," Ramona said. "Just as we used to."

"Life for me at the school goes on as ever it did," Clara said. "Just less children each year. For you it must be so different."

"Is not each period of your life different? Each age, Clara?"

"I suppose you are right. My school period is, well, carries on, unchanged."

"But it was different before," Ramona said.

"It was different before," Clara agreed, reliving for a moment times before Ramona, times unknown to Ramona, times she thought Ramona would never know, and was wistful. She was brought back to the present by Ramona's words.

"... and even here he is on my mind."

"Sorry, Ramona, I was dreaming."

Ramona turned to her and realised she had not listened. "The man I have met. Even here he is on my mind."

"Who?" Clara asked.

"Don't tell Maria," Romana warned.

"Why not?" Clara asked.

"I don't know. It's Alistair's lawyer," Romana admitted.

"Not the old man I handled the copyright with!" Clara was astonished.

"No, Clara. Not him. Of course not him...his son, Mortimer."

"Tell me," Clara softly invited.

"I hardly know him. That does not matter. Not a flash like Carmen and Alistair in the book, but he grows on me. I just don't know whether he grows on Maria too." It was now Ramona who looked wistful, but Carla remained silent, allowing her to speak. "I can't talk to her, silly, it's embarrassing, and I think she can't talk to me, I don't know, she wrote a stupid email, was maybe trying to say something, maybe let him choose, at least that's what she said, my best friend, it doesn't work like that, does it?"

Clara answered her. "The Maria I know is telling you to trust her, that if things do not go as you wish, it is not her choice, her blame. And she is right?"

"You're right, Carla. It would be too foolish for this to be one of the love triangles in my stories. Real life is more prosaic, I hope."

"It is," Clara assured her, but thought of how desperately wrong things can go.

"I often think of an alien encountering our culture, books, films," Ramona continued. "The alien would think humankind lived for murders. I don't know anyone who's been murdered. He would think we hardly eat, drink a lot, and that beds are only for sex, which he would assume to be some kind of sport like wrestling, an emancipated sport in which the female of the species participates." Ramona stopped for a moment and then added, "And then he would encounter the real world and believe there must be another, extinct species, the one in the films, just as the Greeks had their gods on Mount Olympus. He would see us eating, sleeping, sitting vacuously before the television, yakking into a strange instrument held to our ears."

"Cynicism belongs neither in these hills, nor in your books, Ramona. I think you are confused, I think you are falling in love." They both broke into laughter.

That evening they dined outside in the cool air of the courtyard under the orange trees. Fresh Spanish olives, Mediterranean fish and smooth Rioja blended with the Spanish dusk and drew them back to earlier years when they had sat here together.

"It is so peaceful to be back here in this place I know so well," Ramona said, "So real, so far from it all, so familiar and yet so different from my life now."

Carla picked up the copy of *Ramona* from the table and started to read.

Ramona did not know where she came from: she knew neither her parents nor her precise age. It was early spring in the square beside the Cathedral of Seville, the air heavy with the soft scent of orange blossom. The little girl sat among the orange trees...

Clara looked up at Ramona, amusement in her eyes, and then continued to read.

The Reading Group
And there was amusement in Pam's eyes as she chose to interrupt Ramona's words.

"Ramona! You're cheating! Don't tell me that *Ramona Part Two* is going to be Clara reading *Ramona Part One* to Ramona."

"I don't think you'll get away with that, even if you are famous now," Vera advised.

"That's like the play *Noises Off,*" Gloria suggested. "You see the rehearsal, then the same play from backstage, how the actors argue and so on, then the same thing performed - at least I think that's how it went - so you know the reasons why the performance doesn't come out the way it should, you've got to know how the actors' disputes, jealousies and foibles backstage mess it up on stage. It's years since I've seen it. Maybe it's not quite like that, but you do get the same play three times, I think."

"Nicely summed up, Gloria," Ramona said. "The answer is no. Those opening words of *Ramona* were the only ones you will hear."

"Thank goodness," Pam chipped in.

"*Part Two* is not *Part One*, though I like the idea, would have saved me a lot of time and effort." Ramona laughed with them.

***

Ramona
Ramona caught the Piccadilly Line in from Heathrow, back from the Sierra Morena into the subterranean world of inner London's commuters, fluorescent lighting, pallid ill-health, the meaningless babble of advertisements displayed at the rim of the train's bowed ceiling, baggage crammed into the aisles by hapless tourists, swaying and jerking in the world's first, therefore most ancient, underground system, hot, stifling. Never again, she thought, as she stepped out at Knightsbridge station, rather forty quid on the taxi, one third of the cost of my flight, a fraction, less than even a hundredth, of the distance.

Instead of turning right to go down Brompton Road, a decision of the moment took her down Sloane Street and into Belgravia. This is an extraordinary year, she thought, hardly a drop of rain, beautiful days as we know them in the Spanish spring. I am glad to be home, London home, but she did not go home, not yet.

Mortimer was surprised to see Ramona. I thought I would drop in, she told him, since I missed the Cambridge trip last week.

"It's strange, Mortimer, you know my parents better than I. How are they?"

"Well. What can I say? Alistair is Alistair and Carmen is Carmen."

"You are so expressive, Mortimer." They laughed together as the secretary came in to offer tea. Ramona gave her a glance and turned back to Mortimer.

"At this time at home in Spain we drink red wine. Then we have siesta," she said.

Mortimer thought of his four o'clock appointment, did a quick calculation, obliged, and for the first time his secretary served red wine at three, and then at three forty-five she complied with his most unusual request to cancel the four o'clock appointment. On her part Ramona, for the first time, enjoyed to sink into the blue velvet sofa, just a moment's suspicion arising in her mind as to its purpose, but she knew Mortimer to be a gentleman.

Mortimer's business posture had fallen away, his interest awakened by her early life: part of his own family history was their involvement with Alistair's disaster that had turned into this strange tale. She talked of her life in the schoolhouse, of Maria, and it was strange for him, strange that she had no family relationships all those years, yet somehow those she had seemed so family-like, Clara, Maria, mother, sister, almost, as if what was missing was not missing. He was intrigued to hear her talk of Carmen, but she did not. He knew the story of *A Melody of Sadness,* the copyright, the contract, and was intrigued to hear her speak of this, but she did not. And when she had finished, he wanted to tell her about himself, but he could not: he had not cancelled the five o'clock appointment - he wished he had - and his secretary let him know he was expected in the conference room, they were waiting.

As she followed the route back from Belgravia to Knightsbridge, becoming a familiar route, Ramona dreamily recounted the afternoon to herself, thought of what she had said, what she should have said, wished she had said, what he had said, had not said. I think Clara was right.

The flat had transformed itself into an operations centre. Maria was conducting her own single-handed Blitzkrieg, launching her forces against film studios, agents, actors, technicians; whatever she felt had to do with the film. Extracts from the Internet, faxes, notes of phone calls, draft contracts, technical specifications were arranged by category on chairs, tables and the floor in a controlled frenzy of activity. But as Ramona stepped through the door, Maria signalled an Armistice.

"Ramona, hello. Don't worry, this will all be over as soon as the structure's in place."

Ramona dropped her shoulder bag and sat on the only uncluttered seat in the room, an inlaid rosewood chair with arms, surveyed the carnage, the need for battlefield triage.

Maria lowered herself to the floor before her.

"I saw the script as you and me," Maria said, "but Carmen has better ideas than me."

"Carmen?" Ramona questioned, "I thought you wanted her to perform."

"I do, but she's offered to work on the ideas. I'll map it out and show you. We know where we are now." Maria always knew where she was, was Ramona's opinion, unvoiced opinion.

"Your plane was late?" Maria asked.

"I dropped by Mortimer's," Ramona said casually, as her face suffused with red, and Maria exploded into laughter.

"My Ramona, my older sister. Don't worry I won't tease you." God, I wish that email had never left my machine, she thought. I should confess at the Brompton Oratory.

"Get changed. I'll sort out the mess by then. I know you don't like it, Ramona," Maria said.

"And in penance you will cook," Ramona informed her.

CHAPTER FIFTEEN

A GENIUS OF OUR TIMES

Ramona
You have read *A Melody of Sadness?* So you know my story? Was that my story? Does it matter now? Yes, it is true that I, Alistair, went through a difficult period those first few years in Cambridge described in the book, but surely it could not be otherwise in those circumstances, my dire circumstances. Even then there is still a life of the spirit, a quota of happiness to be won, a satisfaction in that once had, even if lost, hope. Was Carmen, when we met that day in Cambridge, captured in the book? Yes, but a reflection, so lifelike but unreal - there was so much more. Reach for your reflection in the mirror and you strike the hard glass, listen to it, it is silent, turn away and it is lost - no, there was so much more, so much more and so much less than in the book.

I remember that first meeting with Carmen in the Anchor. I remember those years of gaiety, the fun, and then her fondness of the beautiful child, and her passion for singing. Can this engender Ramona's *A Melody of Sadness?* As a book, yes - I published it after all - as a chronicle of my times, no, definitely not. I saw tremendous artistic merit in the book, literature is my profession, and never expected for one moment to be dragged into this biographical mire brought by fame - I used to laugh when challenged if it was me, but now the book points like the finger of ridicule, because my daughter wrote it, so it must be true. What is true is that my grief at that time of loss was not a *melody* but the screech of fingernails on the blackboard; it was not *sadness* but the bowel rending Samurai sword and it looked like *The Scream,* but I would entitle it *The Shriek.* Well done, Ramona!

Let me return to Carmen, and if you ask why, then I answer it is because of the film, the film we will now make, the film I am using my money to make. How can you capture Carmen on film? A butterfly in a glass case? Preserved forever, for all to see, when they wish? Carmen plugged into your video machine? No, it is not Carmen you will see, but *Clunk.*

Let me tell you about Carmen. I think that the true Carmen is the Carmen of the Buenos Aires years, and it is my regret that I never accepted her invitation to visit her there, and I think I did not accept it because I was afraid of what I would find after all those years apart. This was a life when she invested her persona in her performances and grew from good to great. I imagine her, the superbly cut diamond I knew, now crafted as the centrepiece of a glittering tiara - these were the reports I received from Buenos Aires. She gave up so much to return here, and was so brave, yet surely this is Carmen: she had achieved what she set out to achieve, and would move on, or in this case return. I think it is true, and I respect her for this, that she felt she must be what she had chosen to be, even if that meant giving up so much that we had, her instinct.

And I see her instinct again in her immediate attachment to Maria, which has led to the film, this strange girl Maria, who has been brought into our lives by our daughter Ramona. This Maria who emerges from nowhere, captivates Carmen and entwines their ambitions in this grand project, this mysterious project. They seem to see what I cannot see, at least until they have made Clunk, and painted their dream in binary digits, for machines to reconstruct for the rest of us in streams of photons reflected off a screen. Did I say reflection? Carmen, Maria, your perfumes, your touch, where will they be in the film?

I have never been a man to dwell on the past, which those of you who have read *A Melody of Sadness* may be surprised to hear, but my anticipation of the future is in my projects, my academic interests that I pursue with drive and ambition: it is not the enveloping enthusiasm which carries Carmen forward or the damburst that is Maria, the Maria we hardly know who is leading us headlong into the assault. And now I will admit it, that I am right up there with them, my academic gown billowing out behind me, as I pompously thrust and crossing-'t's-and-dotting-'i'-edly cut, up there in the thick of battle with them, the third member of the phalanx.

Do not accuse me of pomposity: I have earned it - my work my reputation my position. But now I feel the excitement of the little child at Christmas: after all these years of grind, now at a stroke I shall be a mogul of film, and I cannot help smiling as I think of my colleagues' faces, when I accept with grace the compliments of royalty, rock stars et al at the film's première. I wonder if I can persuade them to have it in Cambridge. Is this the curse of wealth?

And in all this I have not once touched on the real reason why Carmen is here in Cambridge with me, not mentioned the truth, which has nothing to do with Carmen the performer, the film, the professor. You know that Carmen came back to live with me and that is the real truth, that is enough truth, not jewels, tiaras and Buenos Aires. And if you want to know more, then I suggest you ask Carmen.

What I am saying is that Carmen's genius, and that is the word I feel obliged to use, is separate from her human truth, and I expect that the same is true of Maria, but then I do not know Maria and neither does Carmen. Am I being vicious, or mean, when I say that Ramona has a human truth, but no genius? But Ramona is not here to claim that it is she who has brought us to this point, that she has earned fame with her book, that she will be the reason our film enjoys support (before it is made, while it is made, after it is made), she, recipient of the prize for literature. No, Ramona, that is the world in which I live, the world of reputations, of merit by rank, by seniority, by fame: it is not the world of genius, Carmen's world, Maria's world, not ours, Ramona.

You may find that my writing of this is laboured: it is, for I am writing of me, of Carmen, not of my literary subjects I am so comfortable with and accustomed to. I see these two intellects, Carmen and Maria, on the terrace below, outside in the sun. I will join them and thankfully this introspective narrative will be over. I descend the oak staircase to the hall below, panelled also in oak, and furnished in green leather coloured by the reflection of the light coming through the stained glass windows above the door. I stop by the door to the terrace, for a moment. Are they talking of the film? I listen, and they are talking of the film, and then they are still talking of the film, and then they are not, they are not, with Maria's words, surely they are not. "Alistair is a clown," I hear Maria say.

"He is a professor of English literature," Carmen counters.

"He is a clown."

"He is my husband."

"But he is a clown."

"And that is what we need in the world, Maria."

And it is then that I realise Maria is complimenting me, that I, professor of literature, am not cocooned in my chair of the university. I step from my hidey-hole of the oaken doorway onto the terrace to Maria's effusive greetings (I would normally still be in college at this hour).

I join them at the white-painted filigree aluminium table, and I prepare to give them a structure for their genius to wreak its work upon mankind. I explain to them that the technicians, the specialists, the actors, even the directors are not important. First is not even the structure of the film, I say. First is the concept of the film, the vision we wish to create, the imagination we inject into this fantasy world we create, a world for our audience which gives them a new truth, a new vision, a new experience. I am proud that I have, earlier, helped them steer clear of becoming bogged down in the linguistic battle for the source of the gipsy myth.

"Yes, Alistair," Carmen says, with a long-suffering look, and in that moment I realise that everything I have written above about genius is correct. From now on I will take orders - I have so much to contribute, I realise, as long as I do not use my initiative, no that is wrong, as long as I understand where the direction of this project lies, and use my initiative where I am directed. I have no doubt now that all I have written on genius in the words above is correct.

I cough and say, that was just a joke, I'm sure you understand, and they laugh. The discussion continues, and Carmen gladly saves face for me in front of Maria, while I pledge to myself never again shall I plunge blindly into the depths of a discussion ice-cold to me, not with *Clunk*.

CHAPTER SIXTEEN

SOME THINGS ARE BETTER LEFT UNSAID

Ramona

Ramona chose the day of Maria's trip to Cambridge to invite Mortimer to lunch, lunch at home in the flat. She regretted it from the moment he arrived: too personal, too intimate, and therefore too strained. Flustered she apologised that Maria was not there, but had gone to Cambridge, which made it worse, because she suddenly felt she was admitting her subterfuge in the very act of denying it. For his part Mortimer had been harried by the withering looks of his secretary from the moment, when checking his diary, she had come upon the appointment he had recorded himself in defiance of her control over his diary. Why should this bother me, he unsuccessfully asked himself. Yes, she is one of *the ladies of the blue sofa*, a term she had coined, but I owe her no obligations: she like me is young and unmarried.

So Mortimer related to Ramona the results of enquiries he had been making with respect to the film. But was it not Maria's film? Ramona began to feel that Mortimer was more interested in Maria than in her, so she cooled to non-committal replies and dutiful questions, a sensation of ennui, the last thing she had expected, beginning to creep over her. Mortimer began to react to the glaze of her eyes and the discretely stifled yawns, just as most of us do. Urgent work beckoned him to return to the office, to his secretary's surprise. She perched on the sofa, to await his instructions, but she was to find he had none, none of any sort, rather sitting glumly at his desk.

Ramona stood gazing out of the window, as the phone rang. One ring before the answer phone she turned and reached down to where it lay on the table.

"Ramona."

"Yes."

" I don't know how to say this."

"Say it anyway, Mortimer."

"I was just such a bore. I'm sorry."

"Thank you, Mortimer," he heard her voice brighten, and was glad he had called.

"So?" he asked.

"So I wondered if you were free later on," she suggested.

"Where?"

"Make it here, and we'll exorcise lunch, Mortimer."

The Reading Group

Ramona chose this moment to pause to prepare tea for them. Gloria wanted to ask if they would meet Maria today or perhaps Mortimer, but then unusually for her held her tongue.

It was Vera who said, "This is not turning into a romantic novel is it Ramona?"

"Don't pre-empt me, Vera," Ramona said, "but don't worry I don't think I could write one of those."

"Are we going to learn how to make films?" Pam enquired.

"Just let me get the tea. What I will say is there's a really strange bit coming right now."

They sat in expectation, and when Ramona returned with the tea tray, Vera offered to pour once it had brewed.

Ramona

Maria left in the early evening, and Carmen joined Alistair in his study.

"I suppose it is a social norm, here, these days," she said flatly.

"What is, Carmen?" he asked.

"The single mother, no father, you know, bringing up a child."

"What are you talking about, Carmen?" Alistair began to pay attention.

Carmen did not find it easy to say, hence her oblique approach to the subject. "Maria. She wants to keep the baby."

"What baby? Are you telling me she's pregnant, or does she want our baby?" He was mystified.

"She made the most preposterous claim. Doesn't see who the father can be," Carmen answered.

"That's not so preposterous, is it? I mean, well you know what I mean." He gave her a knowing look.

"You misunderstand me, Alistair. She says she's a virgin."

Though she was evidently serious, Alistair could not help but say, "Well, she *is* Maria."

"Don't blaspheme, Alistair. She's serious."

"Well that is preposterous," he agreed. "I've been working with students here for twenty odd years, seen many things, but never that."

"I suppose it's mechanically possible, Alistair. But it's not just that. She simply has no idea."

"Silly accident, drugged up, in denial, lying. That's all I can think of," Alistair replied.

"Doesn't sound like Maria," was all she could say.

Alistair changed the subject, but only slightly, by association. "We'll do a DNA test on ours."

"Alistair, what are you suggesting?" Carmen rose to face him in mock horror. This must be a joke, coming from Alistair.

"As in check the parents," he said.

"Alistair, there has only been you, always only you. Don't be ridiculous."

"Then explain Ramona." Alistair rose to face her.

"What do you mean, explain her?"

"The test said I wasn't the father," he stated.

"That is impossible, Alistair. The test was quite simply wrong or they mixed up the samples. I bore her, so I know I'm the mother, and if I'm the mother, you're the father." Of that Carmen was absolutely certain, so there was only one explanation: the test was wrong, so she added. "Did you tell Ramona that nonsense?"

"Of course not, Carmen. It was my test that I paid for, and what difference would it have made anyway. I mean, it didn't really matter, did it?"

"Well, thank goodness for that. They even amputate the wrong leg sometimes."

***

Later that evening Maria burst through the door into the flat with a: "Hi, girls! I'm here," and was surprised to find not so much the heterosexuality of the assembly, created by Mortimer's presence, as the physical location of the assembly, seated as a pair next to one another on the sofa, listening to music. Of the three, Maria felt the most embarrassed, her thoughts springing inadvertently to *But Gentlemen do not Talk?* She realised how much their lives were about to change, if by nothing else, by reason of Maria's as yet unrevealed, other than to Carmen and in turn to Alistair, situation. In a flash, she interpreted how Ramona might interpret that foolish email, once Ramona heard her news, and Maria turned red, and then she asked herself, how Ramona would look back to this present embarrassment of Maria's: Maria and the email; Maria pregnant; Maria embarrassed to burst in on their intimate evening; Maria and the comments on the deep, soft blue sofa.

"God, I rushed back from the tube and took those stairs two at a time," she exhaled, puffed and panted, as best she could simulate. "Be with you in a tick." Relieved she swept straight through into the bathroom and ran cool water over her red face.

Some things are better left unsaid, Maria thought, as thoughts tumbled through her brain. Temporise? Procrastinate? Some things cannot be left unsaid. She returned to the drawing room where Mortimer sat with Ramona, apparently somewhat less intimately.

"Girls and Mortimer, I have amazing news." She beamed at them.

"From Cambridge?" Ramona asked dubiously.

"As they say in the bible, I am with child."

"Maria!" Ramona looked in total disbelief. Maria, her best friend, a secret of this magnitude, and she could not stop the words: "And what will you do? I mean...who?... I mean..."

"Ramona, no one either of you know, nor will he ever know. I want you to congratulate me."

A multitude of thoughts shot through Ramona's mind, but none of those that Maria had feared, as she stood to hug Maria, totally unsure of what she could possibly say, lost for more than just words in that moment. And Mortimer watched in astonishment at the whole situation, including Ramona's astonishment. How can she not know, he thought, Ramona and Maria, so close, and she can't even guess at that?

They sat down, and Ramona had to express rational words of caution.

"Are you sure, Maria, that you are not caught up with the thrill of Carmen's position. I mean, have you really thought of this - you, us, the film?"

"I'm thinking right now, Ramona, and this is what I think. I have no relatives alive, that I know, nothing for me, everything was borrowed - you, Clara - now I will have something. No let me go on," she waved aside Ramona's endeavour to cut in. "Before this, before our time, I would have been rejected, rejected before, rejected now, lucky perhaps to become the slave-wife of some misfit: now I shall have a child, a single mother, my reason in life, well, apart from the film. You see I can do it."

"I respect your thoughts, Maria," Mortimer said, "but I wouldn't do it."

"You're old style, Mortimer. Fall in love, marry. I grew up with the attitudes of my grandmother's grandmother, probably. Now I can and shall change it all. I shall change it all."

"I wish you well, Maria, but I still ask if this is pride prevailing over sense," he countered.

"Social evolution, Mortimer," she answered, "think of it as social evolution. And don't worry. Just as Ramona had Clara, my child will have me, and look at Ramona!" For the first time in her life Ramona was totally unconvinced by Maria, and still astonished.

Mortimer retraced his steps to his house that night, mystified by the developments of the evening. He thought he had understood these two Spanish London girls, and then this. One thing is clear, he thought: if there were ever any question of it being otherwise, Maria has clearly put herself offside for me. Two impending births in the *Clunk* family: what does that mean for the film?

In the flat by now, curiosity ruled as Ramona quizzed Maria to no avail, metamorphosing through stages of irritation to wistfulness, and crystallising in a decision to keep Clara in the dark for the present. Ramona wondered if Carmen knew, but could not bring herself to ask.

CHAPTER SEVENTEEN

FLUX

In how many worlds do we live at one time? Whatever may be changing in the personal lives of the makers of *Clunk,* the film had its own momentum with Maria driving forward at speed. If Mortimer had taken a step from the world of *Clunk* into the world of Ramona/Maria, or if Maria had taken a step with the virgin birth into the world of Carmen and maternity, *Clunk* neither noticed nor cared. In the battle waged by Maria missiles, guided and unguided, traced their trajectories, lobbed grenades spewed their shrapnel, shells blasted a way through the minefields of vested interest and the bastions of inertia, and gradually the smoke, confusion and dust of the battlefield cleared to reveal what they had achieved: they believed they were in business.

Maria and Carmen determined that they would shoot in India during the monsoon season: for the heavy clouds billowing across the sky; for the deluge descending from above; for the floods; for the transformation of dry valleys to a paradise of flower. This left Mortimer uncertain as to whether they would be taking weather insurance for or against rain. Can we film in the rain, he had asked, or do we insure for the dry and buy studio rain, and the gathering had sought to plug yet another gap in their technical knowledge.

For practical purposes, this meant that filming in India would take place in autumn of the following year. Maria therefore wished to accelerate Andalusia to the heat of the summer immediately before. Apart from the issue of virgin and other births, this gave rise to the question of whether it was really possible to have enough in place to proceed in Andalusia. We do what we do, and we finish there the following spring, Maria determined. Thus, the film had a concept, financing, a timetable, the two principal actresses, and ... well, and that is about all it had, oh, and of course, producer, director, screenwriter. Perspective, perspective, Alistair would say with authority: Rome may not have been built within a day, but the currently held scientific view in Cambridge is that the universe took less.

But then what is it that makes a film? Hollywood has conclusively proved, many times, that money does not make a film. Hollywood has proved that technology does not make a film. What have the French proved? I suggest you ask them. Can you film a stage play? Ask television. The point is that the team was cohesive as regards concept: each section of the musically inspired plot would be introduced by dramatic landscapes set to haunting melodies, before homing in on the human essence of the story, stark but powerful. They would use the power of traditional themes that are available, reproducible and cheap, the power of performance: live on film. Again Alistair would speak with authority: *in arte ars,* and members of his audience would either look blank or snigger.

The team was in effect two overlapping teams: the Cambridge group, Maria, Carmen, Alistair and Mortimer; and the London group, Maria, Ramona and Mortimer, with the entire management and administrative structure falling beneath the London group. The alien tentacles of Clunkworld throttled Mortimer's legal business and encroached progressively on the physical premises of his house; office desks sprang up even around the swimming pool in the basement and Mortimer was driven back in his private sphere to the bedroom. *Clunk* had chosen, after all, to attack the real world, voracious and ruthless, driving poor Mortimer to spend more and more time at the Knightsbridge flat, and in turn Maria to spend more and more time in Cambridge, even when she worked in London during the day. And some human beings believe that it is they who determine their destinies, *Clunk.*

The Reading Group
"Ramona! Alien *Clunkworld*, parallel worlds, creation of the universe, is this not over the top?" Pam suggested.

"And virgin births," Vera added. "How will you explain that?"

"Blue sofa syndrome," Gloria remarked. "Battlefields. I think you're going to have a mutiny right here in this room."

"What I'm showing," Ramona explained, "is how the characters create an enterprise that takes on its own life and influences them in return."

"Like the sorcerer's apprentice?" Vera asked.

"Simpler than that," Ramona answered. "Even mundane."

"Like poor eligible Mortimer is being squeezed out of his own premises into the hands of a female predator," Gloria suggested, anger once again building in her, "but surely he could sleep on the blue sofa, and ... well, OK, maybe not."

"It is amazing," Vera said, "how we seem to have strayed from the purpose of these discussions in these recent sessions of *Ramona.*"

"There I would agree." Ramona looked at the others and for a moment it seemed that her authority would prevail, but as the discussion continued it became clear that literary sense and cultural interest had both fled this particular battlefield, with courtesy likely to be hard on their heels, if the rout continued.

.Ramona

Clunk had spread its tentacles internationally to India and would soon grip Andalusia, but not Clara's schoolhouse in the Sierra Morena, where she led her life oblivious to *Clunk*, to the virgin birth, to Mortimer and whatever it was that he stood for, might stand for, where the children played in the schoolyard as she rested after her day's teaching. But then what did she have to do with any of that?

Checking weather reports on the Internet Mortimer was able to determine that this year's monsoon (he had been following forecasts), had hit New Delhi in India. He had arranged visas for himself, Maria, Ramona, Carmen and Alistair. The question was who of them would go. Alistair decided his commitments prior to the start of the Cambridge term in October were too important, so that left the four of them, none of whom had visited India, all of whom were keen, so *Clunk* obliged. They would play it by ear: get the feel of the place and then pick up some of the Bollywood contacts further south in Bombay, or rather Mumbai now, as they would later learn to call the city, the centre of India's and the world's largest film industry.

***

The city of New Delhi was designed by one of the British Empire's well known architects, Lutyens, on the grandest of grand scales, and even today, in the new millennium, his association with that great city is continued with the activities of a direct descendant, this time in the mining industry. Many grand buildings were constructed in India, Calcutta is known as the city of palaces, often merging concept and detail of traditional Indian and British architecture, of Mogul and British architecture.

The hot summer climate lends itself to high colonnaded galleries, cold marble and masterpieces of ventilation to create a gentle breeze in temperatures above that of the human body. Yet it is a circuitous route that the architectural traditions of ancient Greece and Rome took to India, via the damp and chilly island of England, where such structures do not meet climatic demands. And just as the English suffered the dim light and chill of their vaulted cathedrals and now empty churches, so too do many Indians today sweat in concrete structures designed by northern Europeans. During the monsoon the temperature falls.

In the bookshop of the hotel Ramona purchased a guidebook. They already had one, but the shopkeeper insisted that it was inauspicious for him not to sell to his first client of the day, and he offered her the blessings of his gods, (as she became, in fact, his tenth client of the day). Now she stood under the porch of the hotel foyer and watched the rain, rain such as she had never seen in her life before, a waterfall from the sky. Maria joined her and simply said they would not buy studio rain, marvelling at the torrents. Over breakfast Maria had advised them that this was neither holiday, nor, looking at Ramona, honeymoon, so they would split up to cover the territory efficiently and regroup at lunch: she and Ramona would visit Old Delhi, while Carmen and Mortimer handled New Delhi. The plan to split was a good one, the lunch rendezvous was not: neither party returned much before dinner.

Changed but still looking recently drenched, they sat in the bar of the hotel, deep red velvet sofas, ornately carved and inlaid rosewood tables and on the wall behind a mural, depicting Mogul gardens, geometric beds of plants laid out in the summer heat, long pools of cool water, fountains. A white-gloved waiter laid out a tray of spicy delicacies beside four crystal glasses of blood red liquid, equally spicy, each a Bloody Mary.

"Impressions," Maria proposed. "Let's just give our reactions, to see what we should pick up on."

"Very wet," Mortimer responded. "No but seriously, you've got these incredible buildings. The red sandstone and marble of the Rashtrapati Bhawan, President's place now, I think, palatial, unique. Grand avenues, trees, so much space. Then Conaught Place: sort of like your square in London, Ramona, but a circle and much grander. Streets radiate out, kind of commercial centre."

"So not for the film then," Maria commented.

"No, but listen to this," Carmen said. "They have all these shops, they call Emporia, with all kinds of artefacts, textiles, trinkets."

"You mean to take a look at traditions?" Maria inquired.

"Exactly, and one other thing," Carmen added, "When the rains broke off briefly, this road working gang came out with sledge hammers and shovels."

"And?" Maria asked.

"Well, they were all women. You see what I mean?"

"I see what you mean," Ramona said, "working for a living, just as the European gipsies would camp outside settlements and ply their traditional trades. I read that the clans would take their names from their speciality."

"I hadn't quite made that jump to the gipsies, but yes," Carmen replied. "It's about social structure, and there's plenty of that here. And traditional tools. We saw these women ironing. Huge brass things, must weigh several kilos, that they fill with, I don't know, hot ash, charcoal? And then the best," Carmen started to laugh as she spoke. "There's this group of people standing around, some with bicycles, wondering how to cross a flooded dip in the road, some were wading through, up to their thighs, when along comes, no you tell them Mortimer."

"Can you guess?" Mortimer asked to blank looks. "To get through the water there he is, let's say high and dry, riding, peddling away on a penny-farthing, the old fashioned cycle, right up there sat atop the big wheel."

"OK, our turn. You start Ramona," Maria proposed.

"The Red Fort. Well, three red forts, one in Agra and one in Lahore, seat of the Moguls, various dynasties. The present Old Delhi, one of a series variously destroyed and so on, dates from Shah Jahan in the seventeenth century. This immense sandstone fortress, the intricately decorated rooms. It is so different and yet it reminds me so much of our own Moorish structures in Spain."

"So no good for the film," Maria added, "because we're using the Moorish ones, and our theme is that you got a cultural fusion there, while here it was a time of eviction, well for our people, the ones who fused would have stayed."

"And then the tomb of Humayun," Ramona continued, "a place of power, splendour and I thought sadness too. Also very wet, Mortimer."

"And then the reason we were so late back, I don't know why you were," Maria said. "The driver took us a little out of town, a suburb, to a business that sells antiques, whole floors of the most incredible sculptures of gods, people, wood carvings, religious and ceremonial artefacts, chess pieces, dancing figures and minstrels, erotic stuff, everything. Dating back hundreds and even thousands of years if you believe them."

"I would to a large extent," Carmen slipped in, "There must be so much here for the taking, that it would be cheaper than making it all over again, all these temples, thousands of years of uninterrupted civilisation."

"Anyway," Maria continued, "the one brother, very nice I'll meet him next time, offered to take us out to see some big items at his farm. And now we have something for the film." Maria paused. "Let me say what big items were. They were beautifully carved temple doors, wooden swings to seat three, huge tables, massive sculptures, and then, this you will not believe."

"We probably won't if you don't tell us." Mortimer filled in her next pause.

"You can buy the facade of a Mogul house, you know, the front wall facing the street, a house you'd find in a well-to-do city street. Beautiful red sandstone, carved arches, lattice in stone, sculpted Mogul designs."

"So what's that for the film? I mean we're using the Spanish stuff, you said," Carmen asked.

"If anyone could guess, it would be you Carmen," Maria responded. "You see, I can't take the Alcazar to London or New York."

"Unlikely, and expensive," Mortimer confirmed, with the serious look of a legal advisor.

"But say I buy one of these for five thousand dollars, ship it for five thousand dollars, then I've got a Mogul house front in London."

"Wouldn't match the style of Ramona's flat," Mortimer commented.

"No, but think." Maria made an expansive gesture with her arms. "We load it on a truck, as a float, and parade through London, with flamenco dancers performing right in front of a real seventeenth century facade like most people in Europe have never seen before. Right at the première of the film. We'll get on the national news."

"We won't get arrested by the culture police?" Mortimer asked with an earnestness underlying his jest.

"We'll make sure everyone knows we're donating it to a museum," Ramona replied.

"So I don't think we can do much by way of folklore investigation with this weather," Maria said. "But we got the feel of the weather, which is what we wanted. No studio rain. I say let's not hang around, but go straight on to Bombay, meet the film gang."

Delhi in a Day, India in Three, Maria Travel Services, Book Now, Bored? We'll Accelerate the Schedule. So it was that they left for Bombay the following morning, from the leafy open spaces of the centre of Delhi, the Lutyens magnificence, to teeming Bombay, horns blaring, cars based on a British design of fifty years before (unless of the more modern Japanese and Korean versions), motorised rickshaws, people everywhere, and no rain. With nothing scheduled until the next day, this was the moment to walk the streets, breathe in the atmosphere. The hotel gave onto the ocean, so Carmen suggested they cross through the traffic to the promenade and head north, enjoy the freshness of the sea and then cut into the bustle of the city at some point, see where it took them. And this they did, through crowded streets, broad and narrow, shops, markets, cinemas, the constant to and fro of the traffic, the rickshaws. Then they found themselves, to their surprise back at the sea, a huge stone structure, the Gateway of

India, monument of the British Empire, situated in, they say, the largest democracy on earth, where even Italians can have a shot at being voted to lead the country if they wish, but they do not.

Muggy, humid weather at this time of year, grey clouds above, the fumes of the traffic: they were thirsty and entered the bar of a very smart looking hotel. It was already early evening. As they took their seats, a gap opened in the clouds and the huge red ball of the sun was suspended for just a moment over the horizon of the sea, before dropping into the ocean almost fast enough to see, and the outside world retreated as the windows darkened.

Maria had clearly defined her position as leader.

"Tomorrow, you know we visit the studios," Maria said. "OK, we just look. No discussions about what we do, other than I've already told them."

"You mean no negotiations," Mortimer sought to clarify.

"No, I mean nothing," Maria answered. "We know next to nothing about these people, so we don't want to get accidentally fixed up with the wrong ones or whatever."

"I'd like to talk to a couple of script writers," Ramona said.

"That's OK," Maria agreed.

"You know, get the feel of how they do it," Ramona continued.

"I expect it's stylised. I've seen a couple of the films," Mortimer contributed.

"I've only been to the cinema twice in my life, both times this year," Carmen said, as they looked at her in surprise.

"Well what did you think?" Ramona asked.

"The first one was fun, very Mexican," Carmen replied. "Then I saw one of the new, you know blockbusters, what did they call it again? Well American."

"Did you like that one?" Mortimer asked.

"I think it's very interesting." Carmen was thoughtful. "It was supposed to be natural, the characters, what they did and how they spoke, and I suppose people think it was."

"And was it?" Mortimer asked.

"I'm a performer. In opera we are theatrical, a bit like old style theatre, up to the fifties maybe. But this? Well it's a different kind of theatrical. Absolutely unnatural. That is not how people speak, it's not how they move, it's not how they smile, use their eyes. What do you think, Mortimer?"

"Seems natural to me," Mortimer said.

"This is what's so amazing. As a performer, practised in adopting behaviour, I see it. You don't. It's even more *theatrical* in its way than old style theatre. It's as if you've all been conditioned." Carmen stopped.

Ramona took it up. "You're right. I've been looking at film scripts. It's a different approach, and I've got to learn it, or we'll stand out like a sore thumb."

"Meaning?" Maria asked.

"Carmen's right," Ramona answered. "Take a look at some of the stuff on TV and then concentrate on the dialogue. In some cases they've gone minimal: there is hardly any dialogue, people making expressions, gesticulating, moving, or simply the situation, the visual situation tells you what they're thinking or might have said."

"You see!" Carmen was almost triumphant. "If in real life you spoke like these characters, you'd be considered weird, really weird. Like the old fashioned tall, dark hero. Go around like that and everyone would run a mile."

"Now you point it out," Mortimer said, "I think you may have something. Maybe it's part of the dumbing down process: just see it, don't have to think."

"I think it's more like fashions and trends, what people expect, hero worship," Ramona responded. "I like some of the non-English language films, find it refreshing, because they've escaped the trend, have their own perhaps."

"And some of the new film makers, not yet under the influence," Mortimer suggested.

"Like us." At this point Maria joined in. "We are new, we will do our thing, no one else's. So Ramona, learn to deal with the screen, the effects, but please don't learn to follow any crazy styles of today. We are tomorrow."

"Bravo," Carmen applauded, "Bravo."

Mortimer finished his Kingfisher beer. "Let's see if we can find any Indian food as good as we get in London," he proposed.

The next day they reached the studios in the afternoon, picked up by a white Japanese limousine, out of place in the Bombay traffic. Their host was a tall, portly and very gracious man, seemingly committed to grant their every wish that day. Whether he wished to grant them or not probably made no difference to Carmen. Hardly had they begun their tour of the studios, than she homed in on a set where a young Indian girl was rendering her love song, with dance. Forget about her, Maria told their host, and they had not gone much further before you could hear the voice of Carmen behind them in an improvised duet with the Indian star.

Ramona then asked to see a screenwriter, and their host fixed that up instantly on his mobile phone. They met the host's lawyer, who had just finished a meeting at the studio, which took care of Mortimer, so after just twenty minutes that just left Maria to accompany the host on the studio tour. Perfect, she thought. She told him that she was most interested in his explanations of the technical side of things, how they handled them, and they proceeded to a series of interviews as they progressed through various sets, Maria devouring what she was told, even speaking Spanish on one occasion to a cameraman who had done a lot of work in Spain.

Back in his office her gracious host offered her green tea, which she accepted. His conference table was a dark rosewood covered with smoked glass, as were all the surfaces. Good in the humidity, he told her, as he caught her inquisitive eye, good for those of us who prefer to avoid air conditioning.

"Are you too hot?" he courteously inquired.

"I grew up in the South of Spain, don't worry about me."

"Ah, the hot-blooded Europeans," he responded with a smile. "Bull fights. Matadors. Dancers."

"Just bring me a bull, but while we're waiting," she returned the smile, "let's talk about going on location up north. How you would handle it."

"Be a bit more explicit," he suggested.

"Landscape shots, outdoor dancing, camping, all in the monsoon," she replied. "The real one, not the studio one."

His smile disappeared for a moment. "Pluses and minuses."

"Like what?" she asked.

"Timing, sometimes no monsoon, rain stops." He still looked thoughtful.

"And?"

"We get wet, actors get wet, make-up." He had completed his second list.

"Use the non-run variety of make-up," she proposed. "And the good points?"

"Cheap rain. No need to rent studios."

They then launched into a long and detailed discussion, and two hours later the others had still not reappeared, but Maria turned to him with a smile almost as gracious as his.

"It's a deal," she said. "We'll give it to the lawyers. I don't know what suits you, but I say tonight. I've got mine with me. In fact, what a happy chance, I do believe he might be with yours."

"I'm sorry," he said, "Did I say I was prepared to work with you?" And they both laughed.

A small grey-haired male secretary set out to round up the others, returning with his three charges twenty minutes later. They looked at Maria quizzically when she told them they would dine at the studio that evening, and in amazement when she said she had negotiated heads of agreement verbally, and they would sit down to draft them that very night. Maria and Mortimer will do that, Carmen told her, in view of arrangements she and Ramona had just made for Bombay that evening with the actors. As Ramona and Carmen were preparing to leave, Ramona told Maria that if she were instructed to do the screenplay for this India trip the four of them were on, she should fit it into about three minutes of film to get the pace right, and then suggested they shoot in this year's monsoon, rather than next, and for a moment she thought she saw in Maria's eyes that she was seriously considering the proposition.

Ramona did not enjoy the evening in Bombay. She was glad of the actors, for she felt uncomfortable alone with Carmen, but her mind kept switching to Mortimer and Maria at the studio, to Maria's crazy email to Mortimer, and dispel such thoughts though she may they kept returning. Ramona need not have worried. When they returned to the hotel at three a.m., she entered her room to find Mortimer sipping a whisky, but then it was still quite early London time.

Having achieved more than they had anticipated left them with a day's free time on their hands before their flight back. Carmen intended to make the most of her recent introduction to the Indian acting community, and Maria had one more objective that she wanted to keep secret until she had explored it further. That left Ramona and Mortimer to explore Bombay together, which, though they were not seen at breakfast, presumably they did later in the day.

CHAPTER EIGHTEEN

BENEATH THE SURFACE

Alistair was due to visit the British Museum in the afternoon, so Mortimer, just back from India the day before, asked if he would come down to London in the morning, to go through a few pending business matters that had been neglected as a result of *Clunk*. Maria also wanted to see Alistair, so Mortimer suggested she drop into his office at twelve. He would have finished with Alistair by then and had an engagement (actually lunch with Ramona followed by the cinema).

The solicitors' office was empty when Maria came in, so she walked through to Mortimer's office. Alistair was sitting behind Mortimer's desk, and at first Maria did not notice the secretary, who reddened as she struggled out of the blue sofa. Tough work getting up from there, Maria thought. Alistair stood to greet Maria, and she suggested they go through to the conference room.

"Big boobs, that one," Maria said as they went through, just loud enough for the secretary to hear, but she did not see the secretary's smug look as she returned to her desk. Vexed by her discourtesy, Alistair replied, "And much more. I would take her as a candidate in Cambridge if she applied."

Maria outlined her plan to Alistair, who by this time knowing Maria expressed only mild astonishment.

"That means you want to know about setting up a company in the business park in Cambridge, if I understand you correctly." Alistair looked at Maria enquiringly.

"It will be high tech in the sense of software," she stated.

"But you subcontract out to India, you say." Alistair was not clear about how this worked.

"This is Walt Disney in the twenty first century, Alistair. You use computers to animate now and that means software. What they showed me in Bombay is that there is a huge amount still to be done, huge potential, and they can do it."

"So why us?" he asked.

"Two reasons Alistair: one reason is ours, we want control; one reason is theirs, they want money. Symbiotic, like the crow on the elephant's back."

"I've still not fully understood why we need it." Alistair looked puzzled.

"I think this is very much your territory. Folklore, forests, mysterious gipsies: we are dealing with themes on the boundaries of fact and fantasy." Maria took on a dreamy look, summoning the vision.

"That I understand," Alistair claimed, "but not why we need the animation."

"I want to cross the line now and then Alistair, very subtly, more subtly that has been done before. I want new technology, to be able to drift from our performers into the fantasy world and back without it looking like a cinematic technique. I want Carmen and myself to have a foot in the fantasy world as we perform, cross the line and back, engage disengage, not like against a backdrop but part of that world but as us, not cartoon characters. A dream is real, Alistair, when you dream it. I want this to be as real as a dream. I don't mean like men turning into werewolves, hairy arms, fangs popping out: I mean a wave motion between the two worlds, because that's what I think it's like when you see someone like Carmen perform in real life, and that's what I want to have on the screen."

"Finally I understand your vision, Maria. Why can't we stick with books? Exactly *that* works so easily, just think of E.T.A.Hofmann."

Maria could not think of E.T.A.Hofmann, unable to read German, but she was glad to see that she had won Alistair over to her side.

In the taxi on the way back to the flat that afternoon, after lunch and the cinema, Ramona told Mortimer that she was due to visit Clara for a week, to join her on her autumn trip to Seville. She felt, and sensed in him, that they did not wish to be apart so soon after the India trip, but she had promised Clara and she would go. Mortimer told her that it was probably best, as he would be working frantically on the contracts, instructing the various lawyers they had employed. He asked the taxi to drop them off at the top of Queen's Gate, to walk the rest of the way. They crossed over into the park and strolled along the south side, a grey day, slightly damp, not a word about the film they had just seen, a comfortable silence.

They left the park and crossed through the traffic to walk down to Ramona's square. She climbed the stairs slowly, feeling there was something she should say but did not. As she turned the key in the lock, they heard music from within; Maria was back. My best friend, Ramona thought, for years, and yet everything has suddenly changed so fast: I have Mortimer and she has Carmen, Carmen my mother, so strange. Now we are like two good acquaintances, all in these few weeks. She wondered what Mortimer thought, but he displayed his usual calm confidence, greeting Maria warmly, suggesting they all have tea, and her accepting so naturally. And then there they all were, sitting together drinking tea, talking about this and that, as if everything were the way it always was, just like the first time the three of them met, except then Ramona had thought he had his eye on Maria. Maria the same as ever despite her circumstances, truly amazing.

Mortimer relaxed back in his seat next to Ramona.

"Maria, after tea we will have Champagne, or Cava. We've not yet congratulated you on the huge success of the India trip," he proposed.

"Not me, Mortimer, us, always us." Maria beamed at them both, displaying the joy of her achievement.

"I feel as if I'm in love," Maria said, "walking on air, such a sense of achievement, everything going our way, getting there."

"And you should." Mortimer beamed back at her.

"Yet I have this lurking fear that I will drop back to earth and find the wait unbearable, till we really start shooting, so much to be done. I dread my lack of patience with it."

"That's why we're here, are we not, Ramona."

"Then I *will* ask you, Mortimer, more than a favour." Maria turned serious. "Can you find another partner to take over your normal work? We need you."

"Ramona?" Mortimer turned to her.

"Mortimer will," Ramona confirmed. "He's with us."

Maria stood to give them each a hug, and Mortimer headed for the kitchen, to return with a couple of bottles of Champagne and three glasses: celebration of success, end of an era, start of a new era, an evening they would remember.

Maria was warmly received by Carmen in Cambridge the next day. For Carmen this was to be the first day of their real collaboration. They had agreed that they were well ahead of schedule on the business side, so a top priority was to learn to perform together. Carmen was in charge of this exercise and she had very clear ideas about where they were going. This first session would be three days during which the only interruption would be an hour each day with the voice trainer Carmen had engaged for Maria. Carmen was used to intense pressure and wondered how Maria would react to the schedule she had devised.

The weather had turned unusually mild, and given that most of the film would be shot outside, Carmen took this opportunity to take to the lawn. If Jules, the painter next door minded, he kept quiet about it, as their voices echoed across the beech hedge, trespassing into his grounds and probably into his house. This was not the performance he had heard in the conservatory: this was the incessant, repetitive staccato of practice, the screech of the bow across the violin strings, at least to start with. Tough routine, willpower would be demanded now, replacing the euphoria of their performance in the conservatory: they had a long way to go and hard, intense work to get there, for there is no talent in this field without application. Carmen interspersed voice sessions with acting, the lithe, swift movements she would use on the stage, the flamenco poses she would hold, back arched, head high, proud, grand gestures, seductive glances. She was a master of control for effect. Conveying this to Maria reminded her of the old days in Paris with Caroline. Her physical fitness and stamina gradually left Maria behind, Maria the athlete in Ramona's household.

If Alistair returned home early by design, to witness the action, he failed. They had already retired to the conservatory, now infused with red light from the descending sun, where Carmen and Maria reposed on the rattan seats among the plants, interspersed with Indian figures Carmen had brought back with her. Alistair's mood, buoyed by the long vacation, was spirited in anticipation of the Michaelmass term, with the return of students he knew and the year's intake, the freshers. Carmen was similarly energised by the outdoor exercise and Maria's flame was still alight in an exhausted body.

"Let's get some air. We'll have aperitifs outside," Alistair declaimed, meaning by aperitifs, the word he used for these continental ladies, sherry or Champagne at this time of year, Pimms in the summer. But a corner of his eye caught Maria's relaxed posture. "What did I build this conservatory for? Let's have them here. I'll get a bottle." While he was out Carmen put on Beethoven's eighth symphony, driving out the newly installed Indian influence. Alistair returned, the Champagne cork popped and he poured them each a flute.

"Shall we talk about structure, Maria?" Alistair had been thinking about this on his way back from London the day before.

"I would love to, Alistair. We must." Maria, too, was keen to develop this.

"You talked about animation, cartoons, Maria," he began. "Think about them for what they are, in fact just the same as a film, a series of stills run at high speed to trick the eye. Now think of those great classical painters who painted a whole story in a series of panels, if you like, the other end of the extreme. What if we do a compromise, a limited number of static scenes, but which set out the whole thing? What I am trying to say is that we will then all know what it is that we are working on. We will all be working on the same thing, not going off on tangents and then meeting up to discover we've got nowhere. We'll all understand the structure, the direction, even the mood."

"Excellent idea," Maria said and Carmen nodded in agreement. "It's rather like when Carmen and I were talking about the plot, but had such different ideas."

"I like the visual angle," Carmen added. "It's so much more definite. Less opportunity for the imagination to run astray."

"So what you're saying," Maria interpreted, "since this is after all a family venture, that we should play Happy Families and invite Jules the Painter over."

"You know, that hadn't even occurred to me." Alistair grinned broadly at the thought. "But why not? After all, my money's no object in your hands."

As Alistair and Carmen disappeared to cook, Maria mused, another character stepping on the scene. Is this getting too complicated? What role will he really play? I think the answer has to be that we keep him a step removed, operate him through Alistair, instruct him through Alistair, control him through Alistair, a sort of subcontract. I like the idea of the film laid out for all to see, maybe ten, maybe thirty critical visions. We'll do musical snatches for those bits too. Then we'll start the real work.

Over dinner Carmen reminisced, the days in Buenos Aires, the punishing schedule she followed. They may think the life of a star is glamorous, but she lived it and knew it could be the toughest of professions. She told them that her relaxation was reading. Though she may work late into the night, she would arise in the morning, breakfast and read before anything else. She worked through all the Spanish classics, the South Americans and then the Portuguese and colonial writers. Then it was the great European works in translation. After that where to go? Modern writers, she told them, and how difficult that is but how wonderful it can be, but always finite, always the need for more - they simply did not write fast enough.

"But you, Alistair," she said, "can afford to be a literary snob. You need not read: you can research. You can research some esoteric detail of a classical work and build a whole reputation, life and thousands of pages around it. We readers cannot do that."

"Wyswyg," Alistair said, "that's you, but someone has to look behind the veil, and that's me."

"You know he's right, Maria," Carmen answered, "but is that the job of the English professor or the psychiatrist, the artist or the scientist?"

"I am flattered, Carmen. No one has ever called me a scientist." Alistair looked pleased.

"I think you are a very clever scientist, Alistair, a scientist of literature. You examine it, investigate it, take it apart, reconstruct it, but you never write it. You are the scientist, and I am the artist, like Maria, but I am also a scientist of song, as Maria will be a scientist of film."

"You are right, Carmen, and yet perhaps you are just redefining concepts, definitions." Alistair replenished their glasses of port, and the flicker of the candle was reflected in the polished surface of the mahogany table. Maria gazed at the candle, detached. "I am trying to understand it, Alistair. That is all. You have so much to offer, so much that has been dried and preserved, so much of all the things I love. What I have is different: it is not the flower pressed between the leaves of the book, so beautiful years later; what I have is there for you, wondrous in that moment, and then gone, lost to all but memory, which fades as the years pass."

Alistair was moved, sought a response, but as he searched his mind, he was distracted, distracted by the sibilant sound of the snore, from Maria's seat, well, from Maria.

***

Ramona would awaken each morning in Seville and count the days left before she would return to London, like a prisoner making strokes on the wall. Now it was the evening of the fifth day in the city, two days to go. She sat with Clara, several floors above the city on the balcony of Uncle Fernando's flat, just she and Clara, the others out at dinner. The background noise of the city rumbled below, its lights spread out like a carpet of stars; above in a deep blue night sky, tinged orange by the lights of the city, a fine crescent moon gleamed white. Warm evening air bathed them, as they sipped chilled white Rioja, gentle, mellow.

It was the first time that Ramona had seen Clara since the school had closed. They talked of Clara's plans, which were as yet unclear, and perhaps this was the opportunity for Clara to visit them in London, but she did not seem enthused by the idea. This huge change in her life did not seem to affect Clara greatly, but that was Clara, at ease with herself, her situation, and interested in life around her. If it were not her school children, it would be something else. Ramona was relieved at Clara's equanimity, even though she had expected nothing else from Clara, the Clara she knew, Clara her what? Older sister? Aunt? Maybe older friend now.

Clara knew nothing of the film, nothing of the trip to India, but she was learning much about Mortimer, who was seldom from

Ramona's lips. Ramona felt it was time to tell Clara of the collaboration with Carmen on the film, but her thoughts strayed back to Mortimer.

"It's crazy, such early days, but I'm worried he'll ask me to marry him," she confided in Clara.

"That's not what you want?" Clara asked in surprise.

"I'll accept, Clara. I'll accept and that's what worries me." Ramona sighed.

"Why? I mean why worry, not why marry?"

"The idea is so foreign to me, so sudden ... but it's so inevitable, I think," Ramona responded, uncertainty in certainty. "We're thrown together in the ...," she stopped. This was not the time to bring up the film, "... in our lives. I hardly see Maria now."

"I'm quite sure Maria has her own things to do." Clara adopted a motherly attitude.

"You're right. In truth, it's mostly Maria who's away. I imagine you're right. It would be me who would be lonely, if it weren't for Mortimer."

Ramona brightened up. "Clara I can't believe this bottle's empty, I'll get another, they won't be back for at least an hour."

The next day they all went down to the sea, to the point where the Mediterranean and Atlantic meet, separated at the shore by a narrow stony spit, blue seas on either side. As a child Ramona remembered how she had run across from one sea to the other, to bathe in these famous expanses of water just a few footsteps apart. This was a rare outing today, with Clara, Fernando and her cousins, an opportunity to talk of the different lives they led, their aspirations, their friends. Though so recent that she had lived here as a child, it was all so different now, still Spanish but modern. Her youngest cousin was fourteen, and Ramona thought how strange it would have seemed to her, Ramona, at the age of fourteen to meet someone like herself today, from a different life in a foreign city, and then she had a flash of Carmen at just seventeen and had to smile at her thoughts of changed times.

It was a beautiful time to be there, now that the summer flood of tourism had ebbed and the weather had cooled. And there was energy and excitement in their group, verging on raucous as they moved on to lunch in a restaurant, a good formal Spanish lunch to ensure they were prepared for the siesta. Now was the time to talk of *Clunk*, but how could she when she had not even mentioned it to Clara? But she did mention it to the cousins when Clara took a walk with Fernando, and the excitement escalated, not just a film but to be shot on location here. The after-lunch table was suddenly occupied by actors, singers, dancers, or failing these, budding film extras. But then Maria would not have a choice, would she, other than to include them all? Each and every one of them, and she would want to: it was their film.

***

In London, Mortimer was at his desk reviewing comments received from India on the Heads of Agreement, final comments before expected signature. Light shone in from the window behind giving a golden sheen to his hair, reflecting from the polished surface of the desk and brightening the room. Alert and working hard, he was nonetheless despondent, something missing in the days that Ramona had been away in Seville. She called in the evenings, but that was different. He did not look up when his secretary came in, although he did when she continued to stand before him. Though by no means timid, she did not usually have such a steely look in her eyes. She would be bold, she had told herself.

"What is it, Mortimer?"

"What is what?"

"That we don't … you know what I mean." He looked at her surprised, and she continued, "Is it her?"

"Who?" He was still surprised

"The Spanish girl, Maria."

"That is not your business, my private matters," he retorted, not sharply but firmly. Still he had stung her to a response she should never have made.

"Private! And what hangs between your legs. You're telling me that's public!"

He stood up and walked around the desk to face her. She turned as the light from the window blinded her, and they stood side on to the window face to face, the blue sofa behind her.

"I am sorry," he said. "Look we are both mature, we knew what we were doing."

"I, then little more than a child," she countered.

"You were old enough to vote when you came here," he returned.

"Just. But now three years on, well, I want to know if something's changed. It's fair." He remained silent, so she continued, "I never complained about anything, that you never took me to your house, just here, your girlfriends."

"Well, yes, it is different now. No, it's not Maria."

"So it's ended," she concluded.

"Yes, it has."

"I don't believe you." She squared herself up before him.

"I'm sorry, that's the way it is. We have no claims on each other."

"I will only believe you if you tell me while we ... you know." She looked coy.

"Don't be foolish." Now he was losing patience.

"I challenge you," she said defiantly.

"Absolutely not." This has gone far enough, he was thinking.

She leant forward and whispered in his ear.

Mortimer stepped back and stared at her, debating with himself.

"And if I win, then you accept that is the end?" he asked.

"You will not win, so it will not be the end, not yet."

"But if I do?" Mortimer insisted.

"You will not, but if you did, then it would be your choice. I would accept your choice either way."

Mortimer proceeded to win the challenge. As she left his office and returned to her desk she was ecstatic. I hope, I hope, she thought. A little voice had told her to throw away her pills soon after the Spanish girls appeared on the scene and she began to feel neglected, just as a precaution.

The Reading Group

"Wasn't Mortimer a little foolish?" Pam suggested.

"He'd been doing it for three years apparently, so I guess it was routine," Gloria replied.

"I know this is a literary group," Vera put in, "but I would like to comment on social mores, and I suppose that is part of literature."

"Quite right, Vera," Ramona agreed. "We have to be attuned to what's going on."

"Well, what I want to say," Vera went on, "is that I think the institution of the blue sofa is a good thing." She held up a hand to halt their smiles. "What I mean is it's young people together, no commitment. Traditionally, I'm talking about middle class values, commitment was supposed to come first."

"And aristocrats?" Gloria asked.

"That's just it," Vera answered. "They had economic means, didn't have to worry. Maybe we're all aristocrats now, in that sense, but even better, no babies."

"So you want communistic free love, sex?" Pam enquired.

"Not at all. But people like me, we haven't married, in fact I've never really had a firm relationship, so it's difficult. If we don't want to borrow our friends' boyfriends and husbands, what do we do? If a relationship goes on too long, it begins to look like commitment. I for one, that's the last thing I want." Vera stopped, feeling she might have gone too far, but Gloria was getting interested.

"Women in your position want the blue sofa then, Vera." Gloria stated.

"Think of the girl." Vera returned to the safer ground of the book. "She could be with him but she was not bound by him. She could freely look for boyfriends, for commitment, but was released from the pressure of diving into something, compelled by the need for physical gratification. I mean, isn't that the modern way. If so, don't we need more blue sofas?"

Gloria was not to be stopped.

"If an orgy had been organised in the room next door, would we join in?"

Inadvertently, each of them looked across to the doorway, and each of them was fully aware that none of them would step through. So much for intellectual discussion. Their talk reverted to more traditional literary themes.

CHAPTER NINETEEN

MOTORCYCLES

"What luxury, Mortimer," she said as he greeted her in the arrivals hall of Heathrow Terminal Three. "First the tube, then taxis, and now I don't even have to carry my bag."

"No great hardship, Ramona," he said, relieving her of her slim shoulder bag.

"You couldn't wait to see me?" she asked.

"There you have it." He placed a more than friendly arm around her shoulder.

"I love Spain so much, but this time I was counting the days to get back." She smiled up at him.

"Why's that, Ramona?" He returned her smile.

"*That* I will let you guess, Mortimer, or let's assume it was a rhetorical question."

"I have another question, Ramona."

"Rhetorical?"

"Not rhetorical."

"Shoot."

"I was wondering if we should formalise this." He looked at her gravely.

"You have a very English manner, Mortimer. Jolly good idea, I say." She laughed up at him.

"It's not the right place, but I couldn't wait. That's why I'm here." He stopped and he pulled her towards him, to seal the promise.

As they drove into town, Ramona spoke on her mobile to Clara to give her the news, so strange but thrilling for Clara who had only just dropped Ramona at the airport that afternoon, now a momentous day. And as soon as they walked through the door of the flat, Maria knew something was wrong, or rather *up*.

"So *Clunk* has gained its first victims," she pronounced, on hearing the news. "Your wicked past is behind you then, Mortimer," she teased.

"I would say gentlemanly, not wicked," he quipped.

"I expect nothing more nor less," Ramona said, "and should the past raise its ugly head, then I expect no more than that the gallant Mortimer strike it clean from its shoulders."

"Ramona, to be serious for a second," Maria said, "there is some truth here. You, and to some extent I, do have a strange past, things we don't know. Let's take a pledge that we will always hold together, you, me, Mortimer, all three of us. In a sense you will be my adoptive brother-in-law, Mortimer."

"You know," Mortimer took this up, "it is so strange that it only now occurs to me that neither of you know anything of my family, and yet I've always been so conventional about everything. They will be truly astounded."

"So tell me, Mortimer, while Maria gets the Champagne," Ramona suggested.

"Northumberland," he answered. "I think we'd better go there this weekend, Ramona."

"And Maria?" Ramona asked.

"I would like her to come with us," Mortimer replied, "as family. We'll fly."

Mortimer was an only child, born to his parents late in life. Rumour had it that he had a number of half-siblings on his father's side from earlier liaisons, but if so, Mortimer had never met any. Elderly is the word to describe them both, and they took the news with equanimity in the spirit of about-time-too, and were delighted to make the acquaintance of the two young girls, spending most of the weekend confused as to which one would be the bride. Their manor house bore the signs of passing grandeur, though the seven acres of laid out gardens were immaculately maintained by the gardener who had devoted fifty years of his life to it, and was minded to devote another ten, health permitting. No heating system other than open fireplaces, which were seldom lit, was deemed necessary, and this was the only minor blemish for the two Spanish girls on an otherwise fulfilling weekend.

***

"So it was Mortimer who told you," Carmen said.

"Well, yes, really, you know, traditional, ask the father, he's the type," Alistair responded.

"Except he only asked you after the event. I mean after he'd asked her. What about that secretary?" she asked.

"The way of the modern world, I suppose," Alistair answered.

"Not like us." She came across and sat beside him.

"No, not like us," he agreed. "Not a blinding flash of light."

"I'm glad for Ramona, even if she does keep her distance from us." Carmen was wistful as she thought back to that time many years earlier, to their little jewel.

Alistair felt her mood. "What can I say, Carmen? That's how it is, or how it became."

"Then and now, Alistair. It could never have been different. Do you mind?"

"What can I say? How could I?" He was looking older in the fading light.

"And now we have *Clunk*." She brightened.

"*Clunk* and Maria," he said.

"Strange, you are right," she murmured, "Maria. We have Maria. Our little David battling the Goliath of film. I know she's won."

"With your help, Carmen."

"With my enthusiasm, my lava flows of enthusiasm, incinerating all before them." She laughed. "That is what it is, Alistair. Ice-cold, glittering lava, burning red-hot."

"To revert to the subject, I expect Clara awaits your call, Carmen. You know, kind of *in loco parentis*, turned upside-down as it were." Alistair poured them each another glass of sherry.

"She will be in heaven, Alistair."

"All's well that ends well." He smiled at her.

"More or less, but really more," she answered, debating with herself what she should do this evening, always a problem in this small English town, though less so now with *Clunk*. She had switched off from the conversation and entered a contemplative level, to be followed by a burst of energetic activity. Alistair recognised the symptoms and passed through to his study with his undrunk glass of sherry, which would soon be forgotten as he immersed himself in his current project, so current as to be dealing with the twelfth century.

The Reading Group
Ramona paused to sip her water. Her listeners looked a touch bored.

"The momentous event of Mortimer's proposal," Vera said, "and you do it at the airport, get her to meet the parents, deal with Carmen and Alistair, mention Clara, and all just in a few lines. Isn't this a bit, well, short?"

"Maybe Ramona's right," Gloria said, "I mean, maybe, it's not so momentous. With Ramona you never know what's going to happen, or maybe happen, then not happen, or happen differently, if you know what I mean."

"It's a wedding," Pam put in, "or an engagement so far. We all like weddings, the beautiful Ramona, the handsome, gallant Mortimer. Splendid."

"I have to say this," Ramona interrupted. "How strange it has been with this novel. We were all so literary in our approach before, and now we just talk about the story or social *mores*, or whatever. What's happened?"

"I think we're less inhibited," Pam replied, "say what we want, and then with you here, Ramona I mean, it's somehow different. I mean, it's not just the book."

"It's a worm," Gloria stated, adopting a solid pose in her seat.

"Meaning?" Ramona gave them a gentle smile.

"Meaning reality has crept in and contaminated our cosy chats about books," Gloria answered.

"But not from me, Gloria, not from me." Ramona looked at each of them, but they remained silent. She continued to read.

Ramona
Carmen turned her energy to *Clunk* that night. She had never written music, which, of course, she could read, had never composed; yet she spent six hours scrawling a musical score to match Beethoven for its erratic, untidy style, to match Bizet for its catching melodies, and to

match, sometimes, Verdi for its grandiosity and pomp. Why she did this she knew as little as that she could do this, but she knew she had to hear these sounds recorded in black ink, scratches of black on white paper, well, scores. At two o'clock in the morning she faxed her handwritten score to Maria in London, and waited just three minutes before her phone rang. She did not get to bed until five o'clock that night, and could not sleep. At seven she breakfasted with Alistair, and she felt that the forces of *Clunk* had invaded Poland, if not more.

"Alistair." Carmen had an enquiring look. "That chap I told you about who used to come to Buenos Aires. Remember."

"The banker."

"That's him. Totally amateur but wonderful on the classical guitar." Her face took on a look of reminiscence of those days.

"Johnny something or other." Alistair searched his memory.

"I don't know, Alistair. I seem to have a mental block for the moment. Johnny, that's right."

"Johnny ... Johnny. That's it, Johnny John Heinz." Alistair exhaled in satisfaction with his ability of recall.

"He's the one. Yes. I want Johnny John Heinz to play my score." A determined expression formed on the *Kommandant's* visage. How do we find him?"

"Google," Alistair answered, reaching for his machine. Click, click. "And now Directory Enquiries: Johnny John Heinz, Audley End."

"Heinz." A crisp voice answered at the other end of the line.

"Do you remember me, Johnny? Carmen." The melodious voice no one would ever forget.

"Of course."

"What are you doing now, Johnny?" A very non-committal, soft question.

"As many, Carmen, heading in exactly three minutes for the train to the City. Scooping the last spoon of soft boiled egg."

"Then, Johnny, come to Cambridge instead, to meet me and Maria today." Carmen's voice had that soft undertone of humour and invitation.

"I know no Maria," Johnny answered, "but Carmen, I will take your word on her, I would always take your word. In fact, today I close on a major deal, at eleven, lunch afterwards."

"Then send a power of attorney, Johnny. They will mind, but won't mind. Have one of your young guys get the profile for being there, doing it. Give youth a chance."

"You are persuasive, Carmen." He was wavering, and intrigued.

"What's one more deal in your life of deals, Johnny? I'm," she raised her voice proudly, "talking classical guitar."

And Johnny's motorbike took him not to the station, but north to Cambridge, as Carmen spoke to Maria, insisting, though Carmen did not know of Johnny's motorbike, that Maria hire a motorcycle courier to take her pillion to Cambridge, being the fastest way to get there, apart from helicopter, generally restricted in London to Army, MI5/6, the royal family and moneyed attendees of Brands Hatch on Grand Prix day.

Johnny John Heinz. If you had met him you would know. A man who would turn his hand to anything, including acting as a photo model for the well-known drinks advertisement, displayed on billboards, in magazines, on TV. Johnny John Heinz captivating you, with his expression as he sipped from a crystal glass, in the tube, at London Bridge station, in a country pub - you cannot escape Johnny John Heinz. He was the first to arrive, mounted on a Suzuki super-bike, clad in a one-piece aubergine leather suit, guitar strapped to his back. Berserk though Maria's motorcyclist may have been, he could not match London to Cambridge in the time from Audley End to Cambridge, yet he came close behind, cursing to himself on arrival that he did not have Johnny's bike.

Johnny stood at the entrance as they arrived, insisting he meet Maria in person on arrival, if she was coming all the way from London. Still clad in his leathers, athletic, thinning greyish hair, similar striations of age, premature, in his beard, he helped Maria dismount from the discomfort of the ride, shock visible in her expression, a trembling of the limbs, a release from pillion sub-servience, a lack of control she never again wanted to experience in her life, an exhilaration she was glad to have in her past, and never in her future - damn you, Carmen. But Johnny could handle even these most extreme of circumstances, and Maria's very recent M11 past slipped away, as he greeted her and led her into the house. There are fifty-seven ways to ride a motorbike, he told her as he introduced himself, but you look as if you've experienced the fifty-eighth.

"Meet my best friend," Carmen said, as they came into the kitchen, having met, obviously. "Though I admit I couldn't remember your name this morning, Johnny." Carmen laughed.

"No one ever does," Johnny responded. "Johnny John Heinz. Who would?"

"It's just, this is all so spontaneous. I wanted Johnny. Just a sudden thought. And then he lives so close. I couldn't believe it. Buenos Aires. Four, five years ago, maybe, but years before that. And he's here. So that's Johnny. That has to say something, Maria." Maria caught the mood.

"Let's get started," Maria said, " in the conservatory. And I want to tape the whole thing."

"Actually, we write CDs these days," Johnny mentioned, "but if you don't have the equipment, I guess a tape will suffice. First, Carmen, give me access to your email. I have to encrypt a digital signature, if I may, and deal with today's business, before we move on to the pleasures of the day." She motioned to the laptop on the work surface by the sink, and he flipped it open.

"No pleasures, Johnny," she countered, "the Gestapo is about to extract your musical talents, a piece at a time, bit by bit, until you have no more to give."

"I've just hit the *Help* button," he replied from his position by the computer.

Why did Carmen choose Johnny? Perhaps it was the spontaneity of the moment, the need to have a kindred spirit to play what you composed, in a moment's madness. Why? Why not the professionals, the musicians Maria had lined up through innumerable agents at huge cost, not to the benefit of the musicians, but their agents? No, it was Johnny, Johnny John Heinz.

Alistair joined them for lunch, keen to meet Johnny John Heinz, a name he knew, a face he knew, a person he did not. They were already seated at the dining table when he arrived.

"Johnny John Heinz." Alistair reached out a hand to shake. "A name and face well known to me. Glad to meet you."

Johnny rose to greet him. "Likewise, Alistair. A name I've known for years, but a person I never expected to meet."

"Alistair's our financier," Maria chipped in.

"Then you are very unique," Johnny said. "Little British money goes into British films. It's the foreigners who cream off the profits."

"Is that so?" Alistair looked chuffed.

"More than so," Johnny stated. "You know it took Attenbrough eighteen years to get the funds to make *Gandhi*. Then he took eight Oscars with it."

"So we've got the most difficult bit done, then." Alistair looked even more pleased.

"In the sense of a film like *Clunk* not fitting the standard model and therefore being impossible to finance, yes." Johnny watched a flicker of consternation grow on Alistair's face.

"And in what sense not?" Alistair asked.

"A few." Johnny was non-committal

"Tell us," Maria pressed.

"I'm no authority." Johnny was reluctant to embark on this course.

"Tell us anyway," Maria insisted.

"First, even the best of them expect only about two in ten scripts to work, and they take a hell of a lot of work." They waited. "Then the shoot. *Gandhi's* a good example of success; they shot in India, as you intend. You don't want to overrun. They did pretty well: one hundred and twenty one days planned, three days overrun, rain in the dry season caught them out."

"These are technicalities," Maria suggested.

"In a sense. Your crowd scenes will be easy in India, but you'll waste thousands of feet of footage from people waving at the cameras. Let's say you surmount the creative issues and the production issues. Then you've got to get the damn thing to market. Alistair, you must have looked at the financial angle."

"Actually, no. Well, my people have." Alistair was beginning to look uncomfortable.

"The multiple's stacked against you," Johnny continued. "If you spend a million dollars, the film has to take three and a half million before you see a cent, and so on; that's a three and a half times multiple. Then if you want the US distributors, you have to take bucket loads, as in millions of dollars, that very first weekend, or they'll pull it there and then and you'll probably never make another cinema."

"We have the budget for marketing," Carmen said.

"The power of prayer," Johnny countered with a broad grin. "Alistair, you have staked your all, and I admire you for it. I would have spread the risk over five films."

Johnny had not wished to generate this atmosphere of doom, but what else could he have said?

"Then there has to be a solution." Carmen looked thoughtful.

"You have one?" Maria asked.

"At least a partial one. We take on some kind of head finance honcho," Carmen replied.

"Not enough, in my view," Johnny stated.

"But enough for Maria and me, Johnny. You will be enough for Maria and me." Carmen threw him a powerful look.

"I can't accept," Johnny protested.

"You can't refuse." Carmen spread her arms in semi-crucifixion posture and held his gaze.

That was the day the world changed for Johnny John Heinz.

CHAPTER TWENTY

JOHNNY JOHN HEINZ'S STORY

Ramona

I have always been a banker. You may ask why, Johnny John Heinz? I suppose the answer is that I know the language of numbers. I remember as a little child I did not believe that adults could read. I looked at those strange black marks in books - how could anyone read? It was a joke, a pretence of adults, like the fairy tales they told. I did learn to read and then in my twenties I learnt the language of numbers: if I were shown an industrial project it would mean nothing to me until I saw the cash flows, and then it would mean everything; a balance sheet of an industrial project - beautiful. And I played my guitar.

Carmen? Who could not know Carmen if you visited Buenos Aires in those days? Imagine the thrill of meeting her, and then of playing an accompaniment to her while she sang, in private, to Carmen. That was the first time, but later it was no thrill, because it was something we would do whenever I came down there, and I admit I came more often than I needed, something very special, so special that I carried on playing my guitar, when otherwise I am sure I would have long ago stopped (as of course I have done before this unexpected early morning wake-up call) in those years after Carmen. But those days were pure music and joy, and for me that was Carmen as I saw her on the stage and as we played, well I played and she sang, her private pieces, different from the stage Carmen.

What is it about a particular person? That sounds so wrong: it does not convey, how should I say this, it does not convey Carmen, a concept, a philosophy, a mythology, Carmen for me a mythology.

And that is what it was, how it was. I have always known of Alistair, and perhaps it might have been different without him, but it made no difference. So how do you lose contact? And as I think of this question, I know that the question should rather be: how do you keep contact? There is that power that is beyond you, life, destiny, Karma, laziness? I know the answer, as do you, but there is a power that can overcome it, and that was my early morning call over boiled eggs, always two, with toast and salt, and cod's roe, Carmen's unexpected call.

I know I should have taken off my aubergine coloured leather motorcycling gear on arrival, but I did not. Meeting Carmen again was special, to be savoured. And then I heard this motorcycle with its punctured silencer, trying to be more than it was. Poor Maria. Poor Maria riding pillion on the back of the motorcycle, from London. I did not know Maria, but as I helped her off the motorcycle I felt that I knew her. I felt the trembling in her arms, saw the look in her eyes as she removed the full head and face helmet, the mix of terror and exhilaration: terror because she was not in control, exhilaration because she loved it, and that sense of never again, never. That first image must have coloured my view.

You must remember, I did not know why I was here, invited by Carmen. We went through into this amazing room, a glass structure built on to the end of the house, two storeys with a gallery at the higher level. Carmen handed me a musical score, almost illegible, and my heart sank, Carmen what is this? What are you doing? But the mysterious ciphers spoke to me as they came into focus, as their sounds emerged, slowly, and I began, and I have to say this is true, the right word is to play, to play the strings of my guitar, and Carmen's imagination in that moment entered reality, the same reality as when I learned that those strange strokes on a printed page are not a trick of the adults, the same as my numbers, Carmen's composition.

Why did I not go to the City that day? The answer has to be Carmen, but why? I had a major deal to close that day, but I did not go in, Carmen. Yet what is she to me? Does she mean to me? Nothing really. She is like a film star you want to see, enjoy, know on the screen but will never really know, but then I did know her, but then, when I knew her, she was not a star, she was herself. Have I ever separated the one Carmen from the other, the star from the person? Two

Carmens I may have known, but it was just one Maria I helped off that motorcycle, and it has overwhelmed me, that there can be more than one Carmen, and the truth, that there *can be* a Maria, and this is absurd before I even know Maria, but then perhaps I do, Johnny John Heinz.

I had never read the book *A Melody of Sadness.* To be truthful I had never even heard of it, or of Ramona, the writer, and did not learn of the book until later. When I read it, it struck a chord in me, the scene where they meet in the Anchor, and it reminded me of this day, almost as if the first few chapters of that book were collapsed into this one moment for me. If it was true that Alistair had been dealt a hand of aces, then what about me, as I helped this quivering wreck from the motorcycle, glad to be alive, still, in need of support, to be scooped up and rescued from the cold hands of hell? At the same time I noted that hell's architect was eyeing my super-bike with extreme envy - not for couriers, my man. But these were much later thoughts, not the thoughts now as I race home on my super-bike.

At lunch I could not believe Alistair: not the foggiest idea about film finance and all that money to be poured into the one film by untested amateurs with a wacky idea. I mean, what is this guy? No way did I want to tell them anything, but they insisted. I kept it as anodyne as I could, but still, what to do? I had to tell the truth or at least let them glimpse the truth. Now I can't believe what I've got myself into, me Johnny John Heinz, unblemished record, stuck in this farce bent on catastrophe. Well, that's the rational view, but truly I do admire what Alistair has done, and truly, if I look into my heart, I do believe in the film, in Maria and Carmen, and I admit to being proud, against my better judgement, of becoming associated with it. The legal type, Mortimer, who signed up on the deal for Alistair, sounds a bit of a joke, but then he's probably way out of his depth on this one, London solicitor turned film executive.

Will I get out of this alive? Step by step, maybe. I shall have to engineer some kind of sabbatical from my work, difficult but possible, because these jackaroos are going to need all the help they can get, from someone savvy, canny, ruthless. Does that sound like Johnny John Heinz? I enjoyed the music in the conservatory, the atmosphere and ... No, my private feelings are not for public display,

I'm afraid. You'll have to infer them from later events or someone else's narrative. Is that why I agreed to join this absurd venture?

What of film finance, film finance and me? The answer there is that this situation is no longer about film finance, which is the stage at which we farm out the risk and raise the funds. That is all history in this case, and the trick now has to be to control the creative process, the production process, and then to be very, very clever about getting this film to market. This is where Johnny John Heinz will come in and employ all the expertise and knowledge he has gained over the years. Isn't this what I've always done? I think to myself, what I've always wanted to do, what I do. This is what I do. No harm, I think, in a bit of self-hypnosis, ski jumpers do it these days.

The Mogul house front? I can see us all going straight to jail next time we set foot in India. Have to structure that through some anonymous Liechtenstein company, I guess, that rents it to us for the occasion, or Mauritius; even better, it'll look as if Indian's are behind it, exploiting the double taxation treaty. The film distributors? How do we tackle them? Give them a sweetheart deal and hope for the best? Marketing strategies? We've got to harness the creative talents of these two women. Well, we've got the famous daughter, whatever it is that she has written, so that's a start. This bike is a dream, an absurd, lethal dream: nought to sixty at a flick of the wrist and you've started. I think I'd better sell it. And all this production stuff. Has Mortimer really got a handle on it, contracts that work, people who deliver, turn up even? On location in the middle of nowhere and a key player no-shows! Maybe the Bombay side of things is a strength: those guys know what they're doing, I imagine, can redeploy their talents to suit this film. I wonder how many Indians worked on *Gandhi*. The funds are there, so that's one mighty big plus, until they're all spent, control, control, that we do need. I've got to get to grips with this, now that I'm in. Back out while the going's still good? That's not Johnny John Heinz.

Do they really want me to do a guitar piece? Amazing, would be fun, why not? Fix the bad bits in the sound studio, clean it up. The famous guitarist in *Clunk*. Sex scenes with the guitarist? They didn't mention that. Just romance probably. Is the casting really going to carry the film without known names, stars? We should look at getting someone in, a box office magnet. But then I've seen Carmen perform, and if she can translate from live to film, *she* will be a magnet, I have no doubt. Nice, a Jaguar XKR, I'll burn him off when the lights change before he even blinks. Come on Johnny boy, he's seen you. He's ready, and off! Nice work, Johnny. Yes, I look forward to seeing her on celluloid. Maybe we should practise in front of the video camera next time, get an impression. I'd better call this guy Mortimer, talk through where they're at. Film finance? crazy idea! non-starter! losing wicket! Alistair's off his rocker, and now I am. Carmen, Maria, you're going to have a lot to answer for, and not least my demise as a serious player. God, I hope not. Over to you, Johnny. First, I sell this crazy bike, and then ....

CHAPTER TWENTY-ONE

A GUST OF FRESH AIR

Ramona

Ramona decided to take the house in Hans Place and made an offer to buy, hoping that it had been on the market enough months for a low offer price to be interesting, and it was. Maria could take over the flat in Knightsbridge and Ramona would continue to keep her study there for work. That way she would still be close to the park during the day, Maria would regain her privacy, and Mortimer could turn his entire premises in Belgravia over to office space. The pool he only used during the day anyway, and it could be relieved of office usage, which had been inconvenient for both him and the staff who had been shunted down there. Ramona achieved the purchase within three working days, or rather Mortimer did on Ramona's behalf, and then it was just a question of moving the furniture in from Harrods, just around the corner, although that is not quite how it works.

Mortimer sat across from Ramona in the new drawing room, unhung pictures against the walls, no curtains on the windows, sparse furnishings so far.

"Who is this guy Heinz?" Mortimer's expression contained a mixture of distaste and puzzlement.

"Not the faintest idea," Ramona replied.

"He didn't bombard me with questions, rather he bullied me with them. To be honest, things we haven't really looked at. Sounds like he wants to restructure the whole damn thing." Mortimer stood, moving across to the window to look out over the gardens below. Then he resumed. "Frightening stuff, some of what he said. I almost wondered for a moment if I should ever have stuck Alistair into this."

"It was his choice," Ramona objected.

"Really?" Mortimer looked at her in mock surprise.

"You're the lawyer, not the babysitter, Mortimer." Ramona rose and came to his side. "Lovely gardens. I'm glad we did this. Forget Heinz or whatever his name is. And you don't have to worry about Alistair."

Mortimer took a brief call on his mobile.

"Unbelievable," he said, "he just called to say he's faxed back with comments all the contracts I sent up the day before yesterday. You know how many hundreds of pages that was? Seems to have some kind of master arrangement and changes to the corporate structure. I'd better go across to the office."

"You look mournful, Mortimer."

"I am. The good old days when I had everything under control."

If Mortimer felt he was being hounded by Johnny John Heinz, he in turn was being driven by Maria. Suddenly she had someone to really bounce ideas off, someone who could encapsulate an idea in commercial format, and that is just what Johnny John Heinz was doing: pulling everything together in a tight structure, tailored to the objectives, no loose ends, and no play in the joints. He told Maria that he felt Mortimer had done a pretty good job, but needed more instruction from a principal. He had too much rope, he told her, which would now by yanked in. He'll bleat a bit, but we'll get there, he had said, and Maria laughed, as she saw a mental picture of a bleating Mortimer, realising he would find his new principal a little less compliant than Alistair. You know there is a conflict of interest, Johnny mentioned to Maria. Planned in Johnny, planned in, was her response. How else to get Alistair into the deal? And it was Johnny's turn to smile.

The next day Johnny gusted in on Ramona with storm force.

"You've got to understand the difference, Ramona. You write a book, maybe get a bit of editing input, and bang, out to the publishers. With the film script you're right at the bottom of the food chain. Every step of the way a whole series of people is going to come back with demands for changes, and I'll tell you the unfortunate thing, changes for very good reasons. And the redraft's going back into the chain to engender yet more changes. Rule number one: give them the meat as soon as you can. Rule number two: be patient, because no one else will be."

Tough though his lecturing was, Ramona found his manner engaging, and had to accept the truth of his words, as he moved through a series of topics.

"I'll acquiesce, Johnny. Don't worry." Ramona had not said much else. "And I can work fast. First draft in ten days."

"OK, and tell Mortimer, I gather you two are friendly, that he's done a good job. I'm not sure he'll believe me if I tell him, and I mean it. It's not been an ideal set-up, loading it all up on him, but he's acquitted himself with honours. I'm just being ultra-tough, because I have something to add to this, and take no prisoners. It's a question of style, my style.

"The Sergeant Major style," Ramona laughed.

"Nuclear tipped, Ramona, and warp speed." He gave her the famous grin from his posters.

"You seem to have an extraordinary capacity for getting things done, Johnny. Mortimer felt as if a legal team had got to grips with his work." Ramona looked questioningly.

"Focus, Ramona. Do what you've got to do and forget the rest. Skim the boiler plate, slice up the meat, if you know what I mean."

"I don't, but I get the gist. You're not the sentimental type," Ramona suggested.

"Now there you're wrong, just not in business." Johnny seemed about to add something but stopped. Ramona wanted to ask about how he knew Carmen, but the moment did not seem right. He rose to leave, in some ways a relief for Ramona: she felt drained.

In the afternoon Johnny met Carmen in Cambridge, where she was reviewing some work done by Jules, twenty panels sketched out. She explained to Johnny how she saw the mood of the film captured in these snapshots. He told her that Jules should use A4 size paper next time, easier to scan, and immediately set about scanning them and emailing them to Ramona in London.

"I shall be circulating a responsibilities sheet, what each of us will do by when." Johnny looked up from his scanning. "Twenty-four hours to respond with comments, and then the cement sets."

"I'm not sure it's our style." Carmen admonished.

"You're most definitely right, it's not. Maria, liked the idea, though, until she realised she would be on the list. Your style's good for the creative side and has plenty of leadership. All I'm doing is making life a little less pleasant for everyone. Even enthusiasm has to be controlled and measured." Johnny hit a few keys to store the images.

"But you're not on the list, Johnny." Carmen looked at him defiantly.

"Good guess, Carmen, and right. No, I'm not." He grinned. "My life's tough enough anyway."

"No one has ever controlled me," Carmen objected.

"You've never been a film star," Johnny countered. "Carrot and stick all the way, I'm afraid. Some of them think the carrot is pampering but it's not: it's manipulation. The limo to the set is not a courtesy: it's to make damn sure they get there, like kids on the school bus."

"You are being vulgar, Johnny."

"Commercial, Carmen. Don't be so old fashioned."

"Truce?" Almost a pout.

"Once you've signed off on the responsibilities, why not?"

"I'll give you my comments now, Johnny. Call it a timetable and I'll sign off. Agreed?"

"Done." Johnny offered a handshake, which Carmen accepted.

Then Johnny turned serious. He explained to Carmen that he had researched the making of a few films that had been heavy on location shoots rather than studio settings. He suggested they impose a rigid schedule to retain the discipline and also the "heat" of the film. Three months shooting in Spain next summer and then one month in India in the monsoon, followed by editing in Bombay, was the schedule he had in mind. Prior to that they would put the studio scenes to bed. Everything was to be timed backwards from there, and that was what was contained in the "timetable", shocking but achievable. To maintain the early momentum, he had built in a couple of months of break, before they commenced filming. We'll all be ready to go, preparations all done, he told her, and that would give them a huge sense of confidence and control over what they were doing.

Johnny slipped a disk into the computer and printed the hastily renamed timetable.

"There's nothing in here about lyrics," Carmen objected, "my lyrics."

"Come now, Carmen." The famous grin. "I couldn't stop them if I tried, now could I? No need to burden the timetable with redundant information."

She carried on reading. "But I'm not on the list, Johnny." She looked at him in astonishment.

"Did I say you were, Carmen?" The grin broadened and erupted into a low laugh.

"Johnny ..." A touch of the wolverine snarl, but humour took control, and she too erupted into laughter. Johnny left on this note, and just missed Maria's arrival.

The Reading Group

Pam: "I like Johnny, Ramona, but don't you think he's come on the scene, kind of a bit suddenly, and well, late?"

Vera: "I'm not so sure, Pam. I mean, I always found it a bit incredible that these people were actually going to make a film, and now you have someone to take control, Johnny John Heinz."

"What about, Maria?" Pam responded, but Gloria answered for Vera.

"Strength of character, but needs support, experience. I agree with Vera, although I find him entirely unsympathetic. Mortimer's my man." Gloria beamed at Ramona.

Ramona stepped in. "And there's something more to do with the relationships here. You had the potential for two fatal flaws: Ramona and the relationship with her parents, festering; Maria seemingly decamping to Carmen, or pushed by the Mortimer situation, but still in a sense Maria's the outsider and then somehow not, but then she's in charge. Awkward, the whole situation has become awkward, so where's it leading them?"

"And in steps Johnny John Heinz." Gloria gave a grand gesture.

"Yes," Ramona agreed, "in he steps, and perhaps that is why there *is* a story to write and not an implosion. What do you think, Pam?"

"I take your point," Pam accepted. "Better late than never."

"I'm trying to remember where I've seen his picture," Gloria started.

"The book, Gloria," Ramona admonished again, "the book."

Vera busied herself preparing tea, and the conversation drifted on.

"There's a more general point, I've been thinking," Gloria said, "and that is really what comes out in the book. People seem to be able to live with the great crises, adapt to them, like Alistair and Carmen, but it's the little things that niggle and suddenly take on significance, and then it's the dynamics of the relationships that herald change, like Mortimer and Ramona, Carmen and Maria. It's not the plot that's driving them: it's they who are driving the plot."

"Isn't that the way it is," Pam opined. "William the Conqueror decides to snatch the English crown so King Harold gets an arrow in the eye. I mean, it's not as if some arrow materialised out of nowhere, Harold got shot in the eye so William took the crown." Pam stopped, wondering why Gloria was apparently trying to suppress giggles, and then Vera returned with the tea.

Ramona

Mortimer was becoming used to calls from Johnny John Heinz at strange times of day.

"Mortimer, this one's conflict of interest for me, over to you." Johnny's clipped business tone.

"What?" Mortimer asked.

"My contract. I wanted you all to see what I'm about. Now you know, so I want you to agree my contract with the board, and then I'll agree it with you."

"I'm assuming you have a draft in mind, Johnny." Mortimer glanced at his email to see if one had come in.

"Not this time, Mortimer. I'm serious. You guys take a view, and tell me. Brainstorm it on the email, Mortimer. Give them your own thoughts and get them to respond. I think you recognise that the existing structure has, well let's say, a bit of a conflict of interest, in your case. I might be your solution, just in case it get's messy."

This was not a subject Mortimer wished to discuss, so he agreed and hung up, but he had taken the point. Looking at it objectively, he thought, I have compounded a complicated business situation with the personal situation. It could all be construed quite badly, if one were so minded, and they were talking of big sums of money at risk. I am beginning to think I need Johnny more than anyone, were his thoughts, and he has such an incredible nose that he knows it, so he's made me his spokesman, knowing that is how he will get the best deal, shrewd, pretty damn shrewd, as Johnny would say. He is right too about showing us what he is about: no way could he have waltzed in on day one and negotiated what we are about to give him. But then Mortimer was not privy to Maria's thoughts.

Maria faced Carmen in the kitchen in Cambridge.

"The truth is I don't trust him," Maria said to Carmen.

"My Johnny! You're joking!" Carmen looked at her in astonishment.

"No, not in the sense of being suspicious of him, in the sense that he dominates," Maria responded, as Carmen eyed her with curiosity.

"As in weak knees," Carmen suggested to Maria.

"Carmen!" The familiar warning tone.

"Admit it, Maria. He turns you to jelly." Carmen found this highly intriguing.

"Motorbikes turn me to jelly." Maria stood firm.

"Motorbikes and J.J.H." Carmen continued to tease, and Maria began to blush, despite herself. "What you meant," Carmen continued, "is that he's outside your sphere of control."

"Actually, I don't think that," Maria answered. "I think the very opposite."

"So you do admit it!" Carmen's curiosity would not let go.

"Alright, but just a little bit," Maria did admit.

"As Mortimer would say, I rest my case." Carmen decided to wear her triumph gracefully, and Maria was grateful of this dignity, wanted to say more, much more, but did not.

Maria was delighted with the work of Jules that Carmen showed her, so they crossed the garden to see if he was home, to be collected by Alistair some two hours later, with the serious complaint in good humour, that it was not his turn to cook. As they returned to the house, Alistair casually remarked that Johnny was coming for dinner, and Carmen managed to catch the hastily concealed glitter in Maria's eyes. It happens to them all she thought, but this one has made her situation more complicated, thoroughly modern Maria.

Champagne in the conservatory appealed to Johnny, who sat with Alistair as the ladies dealt with the kitchen. Johnny had prudently booked a taxi and Alistair obliged with a second bottle of Champagne.

"I've asked Mortimer to prepare my contract," Johnny said to Alistair. "He should ask you all for advice."

"I rely on him," Alistair answered.

"Not this time, Alistair. Listen to what he says and talk to the others. Exercise your judgement in fairness to him." Johnny adopted a mature man-to-man posture.

"What do you want?" Alistair enquired.

"Shall I tell you something, Alistair, or rather predict? You will give me exactly what I want."

"How can you know? I mean ..."Alistair did not get the opportunity to continue.

"I know, Alistair," Johnny interrupted. "And now *you* know." Johnny's grin broke into his laugh, and Alistair popped the second Champagne cork.

Over dinner Carmen was unable to resist her knowing glances, which Johnny did not seem to mind but which unsettled Maria, who continually brought the conversation to the neutral territory of the film, until Alistair suggested that there was a natural limit to the amount of clunking one could do at a given session. Then Johnny eased the tension.

"Maria, as soon as my contract is signed, and no ulterior motives can be ascribed to me, I invite you to dinner. No motorcycles. Agreed?"

"You drive a hard bargain, Sir. Yes." Maria felt a clearing of the air and her tension ebbed.

"And me?" Carmen asked.

"Risking the fury of the spurned woman, I can't remember the quote, no, Carmen." Thus died Carmen's final tease. The conversation moved straight to the old days in Buenos Aires, and as Carmen and Johnny spoke, the atmosphere came alive for Alistair and Maria, the description of her performances, the haciendas, the life of *her* Buenos Aires. Then Johnny spoke of the reasons for Argentina's latest financial collapse, and his regret that his business in that country had disappeared, not to return for years, gallantly adding that it did not really matter since Carmen was no longer in Buenos Aires.

Alistair brought up the Science Park, and Johnny learned of the animation idea. Leave it to them, he counselled Maria. Maybe give them money, but leave them in control. Leave the entrepreneurial risks with those who understand the situation. Too much technology, change, false starts and blind alleys, he opined. How can we judge who will get it right, them or others? Just stick to the product, not the manufacture: we are consumers not producers of this product; we are on the artistic side not the technological; we pay others for technology; and as he spoke Maria's sense prevailed over her initial enthusiasm. Once again the Johnny John Heinz approach bore fruit. And what if he's wrong, she thought, just a sophist, but *that* she could not believe, as she looked across the table at him.

CHAPTER TWENTY-TWO

THE PUBLIC EYE

Ramona

What is the critical phase in making a film? The answer has to be: many or none. If you do not have a concept, you will not get financing, in which case you probably will not make a film. The simplest way to get a concept is to buy it: find a recent box office blockbuster for which you can buy the rights to the sequel, the contracts of the principal stars and the services of the script writers, and it still might not work, but even when you fail, at least you will get publicity so that you can raise an equal amount to lose on your next film. If you do not have fifty million dollars plus before even starting, you might prefer to avoid this approach.

The fact was that *Clunk* had a cheaper concept and indeed had financing in place, so where should it go from here? Make a good film? Not enough. What does the public want, and just as important, what is the public perceived to want by the people who ensure that films are shown, particularly in the US? Let us say you get all that right. Bingo? Unfortunately, the particular weekend you launch, the public decides something else is more important: an assassination, sports event, earthquake, another film? So you build the hype in advance, to be most important.

This was the big concern that Johnny John Heinz was turning his attention to: how do you build the hype for this unknown commodity? Contrive a mega-scandal involving presidents, cabinet ministers, press barons and royalty? Do a TV series first? Maybe in this case just solidly plug away at the media and hope for the best, take a punt. Is that not what it was, a punt? I simply do not have the contacts in this business, he told himself, and that's probably what we need as much as anything. Can we buy them? Cut someone into the profits for free? Get a mega-backer? Is that what Maria and Co. would want, anyway? But it's down to you, Johnny, you're committed now, and he signed the contract on the table in front of him.

Johnny stepped out of the conference room and back into Mortimer's office. He glanced at a weird blue sofa and opted to seat himself on a corner of Mortimer's desk, sliding a copy of the signed contract across to Mortimer.

"Nice work, Mortimer. One day I may be as rich as you." Johnny grinned at Mortimer.

"Seriously, Johnny, I've got everything riding on this now. I've even passed my legal work to a new partner. Hard to get it back if we screw up." Mortimer looked less poised than normal.

"I know the feeling. Pre-race nerves." Johnny laughed. "If you like understatement."

"They're impressed by your confidence, Johnny. What's beneath it?" Mortimer asked.

"Not much. But remember, fear is contagious, and panic, well panic is terminal." The grin still there.

"So what did you do in the tech stock crash, Johnny?"

"Mortimer! You must be joking! Me, Johnny John Heinz! Wouldn't touch the stuff. You want to know an interesting fact: Lemmings don't drop over cliffs into the sea. That was all based on one completely spurious pseudo-scientific report by a guy who saw a bunch of lemmings migrating seawards, and the roller coaster took off from there to become modern scientific folk lore, only recently disproved. So I guess if it weren't for that guy's mistake, financial markets would behave quite differently when they opt for lemming mode."

"I hand it to you, Johnny. You're impenetrable. Maybe someone who counts will believe you know something about films. I have to confess, I'm beginning to believe I'm transparent: they see straight through me to the money." Mortimer had truly never claimed knowledge of this business.

"Dangerous candour, Mortimer. Let's keep it between ourselves. I'm going to give you a fact file of things to spout when the going gets tough, to throw the opposition. And by the opposition I mean the guys who are on our side. Don't even bother to speak to the others. Congratulations on your engagement, Mortimer." Johnny reached out a hand and Mortimer shook it, beginning to feel assurance of Johnny's goodwill.

"Thank you, Johnny."

"You know you've got me wrong, Mortimer." Johnny did not release his hand, but sat there on the corner of the desk looking across at Mortimer. "Tools of the trade, what you think of as my type. It's just how we do it, and we take it off in the evening, the image, like the business suit, at the weekend. Don't hold it against me. It's not your world, but we'll get to know one another, let's say, outside the office. And you've earned my respect for what you've done here, now that I know the circumstances." Johnny released Mortimer's hand and his grin broadened. "And before that I thought you must be a complete joker, to use the polite form."

Mortimer was used to the more conventional approach, but he detected a cosmopolitan sincerity in what Johnny said and in his manner that left Mortimer feeling much more comfortable about the whole situation. Johnny felt no less adrift than before, just committed adrift now, as he looked at his signature on the papers he had just signed on Mortimer's desk.

The secretary buzzed, announcing Ramona, and Mortimer requested two more minutes with Johnny. He wanted to check through all the papers, make sure everything was in order and give Johnny his copy. *She* looks decidedly sour today, Ramona thought, not her usual buoyancy and glamour. And it is true that she, Mortimer's secretary, was sour, for nature had announced to her that even the best laid plans are fallible, leaving her well and truly out cold in this round, with no prospect of a return match. She was pondering her future, her designs on Mortimer thwarted, the workload growing and those former office interludes gone with no prospect of return. And here was one of his two Spanish girls, the writer, acting like some kind of goddess, and he even lives with her now, she thought, why, why, why? After all I've done for him, always here. Why, Mortimer, why? She glared at Ramona, but looked away as Ramona looked up. Then Mortimer called Ramona in and she joined the two men.

"I have just congratulated, Mortimer," Johnny said. "Here it is bad form to congratulate the lady, as she is evidently so deserving that one would not for a moment wish to suggest that she has done well, so my felicitations, and a continental kiss." He drew her towards him by the right hand, as the secretary scowled through the open door, and performed an imperial Austrian *Handkuss*, a gentle breath on the back of the hand.

"Now that I'm on board I have some ideas. Let's have a seat," Johnny continued, glancing at the sofa, "in the conference room."

"Ideas, Johnny John?" Ramona laughed. "What else have we had from you these last few days?" They went through into the conference room, with Mortimer taking the head of the table, the others on either side.

"Right now, Ramona," Johnny said, "you are the Prima Donna, the one of us with profile, fame." Ramona blushed. "But let me get to the point? We've got to look at this whole thing differently now."

"Fire away," Alistair suggested.

"I remember when I was a school kid," Johnny opened.

"You were a school kid once?" Ramona cut in, as if incredulous.

"On a German exchange. Workers in Frankfurt, factory closing, striking for the right to carry on producing typewriters no one wanted. Even then it was obvious to me that there's no point in producing what no one wants, unless you were a cold-war-fully-planned communist of course."

"I admire your precocious perspicacity, Johnny." Ramona could not resist a little sarcasm.

"So let's make some assumptions," Johnny continued. "Let's assume we are making something they want, one, and two that we can do it. OK, that's the production side and let's say we have that under our belt. Agreed?"

"Carry on," Mortimer suggested.

"That's still no good," Johnny stated. "They've got to know first that it exists and second that it *is* what they want."

"So we're in marketing and sales now," Mortimer said.

"Still not good enough," Johnny paused. "They have to know they want it, where and when they can get it, i.e. that it's available, and now most important, that they want it more than they want the other stuff that's available that they also want."

"So what's the point?" Ramona asked.

"We have to be a *must*. But we have to be that even before our première. We need profile, and you, Ramona, are going to lead the way. We are going to make you a celebrity, then bring the other two ladies in on your coat tails. And you, Mortimer, look the part too." Johnny leant back.

"I think you'd better talk to Maria," Ramona said.

"Johnny smiled at them, "I have. She's asked me to do the guest list for your wedding, which we've scheduled for May of next year." Johnny thought this was a good moment to make a hurried departure with the excuse of another meeting, as Ramona and Mortimer stared at one another in disbelief, Johnny giving the secretary a friendly wave on the way out, a smile on his lips even as he reached the street.

"Hello, Johnny." Maria greeted him later that afternoon at the entrance to the house in Cambridge, in a reversal of roles from that first time. "Do come through. Carmen's not back yet." She led him into the conservatory, her contours revealed by the raw silk dress, shimmering green. Did she expect me? he wondered, hoped.

"You saw, Ramona?" Enquiring eyebrows.

"And Mortimer." Johnny took a seat opposite her, remained inscrutable. Silence.

"Reaction?"

"Shock." His eyes creased into a smile, sought her eyes and held them. Silence.

And Carmen entered with a flourish, a look verging on apology transformed in a moment to one of greeting, and then admonishment for no guitar. Then Alistair was with them, moving straight into his aperitifs routine, to join them seconds later with glasses and a bottle. He turned to Johnny, as he opened it.

"If you've signed, what's the prognosis?"

"I have signed. Now give me ten days, but for the moment, I'd say, yes it's buttoned up, there's a film. It's the far end that needs fixing." Johnny meant what he said.

"I'm relieved, after the first time we met." And Alistair sounded relieved.

"Don't be too relieved," Maria said. "Any film's a gamble. This one less so of course."

"I have a nose for it too, Alistair," Carmen added. "I always knew which performances would flop, but sometimes I needed the money and they paid me anyway, well, except once."

"Well let me just say," Johnny took over, "that Maria has been a commendable Napoleon to her field marshals. But now the action starts, and I'm going to take the practical burden off her shoulders. We're going modular, every bit doing its thing, and I'll ensure it binds together, leaving Maria to work on the creative side now, and then direction and performance in due course. But the big challenge is still the ultimate one: to lift it into the public eye."

"And what we want is free advertising," Maria added, "celebrity, even notoriety."

"I'm not so keen on the latter. We have had a taste," Alistair said, and Johnny was intrigued by the remark, just not sure if this was the right time to ask.

After dinner Johnny spent a few minutes with Maria in the sitting room, waiting for his taxi. He remembered the notoriety comment.

"What was that about, Maria, Alistair having a taste of notoriety," he asked.

"You don't know the Ramona story? You've known Carmen all these years. No, I suppose people don't know the real story." She was thoughtful.

"Tell me, Maria, or should I ask Carmen?"

"Not enough time tonight, Johnny, but I'll tell you. What was that about once you'd signed the contract?"

How could that have escaped him? Amazing. The dinner invitation. "I was thinking of tomorrow," he said.

The taxi hooted, she kissed him on the cheek and said, "I'll be here."

CHAPTER TWENTY-THREE

PUBLICITY

Ramona

It had proved to be an evening beyond expectations, and not just because he was with Maria, the two of them for dinner, but because of what she had told him. As Johnny John Heinz drove into his farmyard, the lights went on around the barn. He had kitted it out with fish tanks and had a business selling all kinds of tropical and cold water ornamental fish, run by a couple of local lads. To the right was the apple orchard and then the white painted walls of his modest farmhouse. He pulled up on the grass beside the front door, and sat for a moment. What a story! Are they making the right film?

Come two o'clock in the morning, he was still in his study in the dark, looking out through the diamond leaded panes into the moonlit orchard. Celebrity or notoriety, she said, and they have this. Incredible. The kidnapping story, the theft of the book, the prize, and, of course, the real story in the end has never entered the public arena. The official version is that she was kidnapped, but rediscovered her father. Do they want the film that much that they would be prepared to use this? Think of the press releases. The interviews with Carmen (remorseful?), Alistair (forgiving?), Ramona (reunited?), kind old forbearing, protective Clara, Maria the orphan. So tragic, but all patched up in a team to make the film. Or maybe, Carmen, the wicked witch, and her tragic victims Ramona and Alistair, reunited by fate after all these years. Carmen standing trial on the première of the film. Limitless.

Would you do this, Johnny? I don't think you would. Will Maria do this Johnny? I think she will. Where does that leave us? She does not have an understanding of family like most of us, probably as a result of her background, but then perhaps it's similar for Ramona. How do you do it? Serialised in the Sunday papers? Then a book? Carmen? A ghostwriter? Ramona? Or is she too literary? No, I cannot do this to them, and I must stop Maria, if that is what she intends. This is not my style. What does Mortimer know? Or not know? Incredible. For the first time I can truly say I am in turmoil, somehow on the sidelines yet involved, more involved with every day. Every day? These few days? You are in the mire, Johnny, in the mire and sinking. I don't sink. He called Maria's mobile. *Please leave a message after the tone.* Oh well, I tried.

In London Mortimer was roused from his sleep. The phone at this hour! It can only be Heinz, damn him, but Mortimer answered the telephone nonetheless. It was not Heinz. One thirty-five, the clock showed, and he handed the phone to Ramona, saying it was Maria, turned over and fell asleep. It was a very long and fraught conversation, which is why Johnny failed to get through to Maria. The gist? Exactly what Johnny was concerned about.

The next telephone call was at eight the next morning, from Ramona to Carmen, a request to come to London to meet, an odd request, do not tell Maria, Ramona had instructed, but odd anyway, Carmen thought, that Ramona should suddenly want to see her of all people. She complied: they would meet for lunch at Ramona's new house.

Waiting for Carmen, Ramona sat in the same seat as she had sat just the day before. Then she had imagined the furnishings she should acquire, the décor of her new home, but her thoughts were far from this now. How much has happened these last few months, how unimaginable, yet it is as if we sit on a knife-edge, our hopes so hard won, so easily lost, that I should now rely on Carmen of all people, she thought, but then maybe not so strange. The bell rang, and it was with an effort that she rose and descended the staircase to let Carmen in, wishing it were Maria, a contrite Maria.

Carmen ascended the stairs behind Ramona, as yet uncarpeted but a splendid rich mahogany. Light filtered through a magnificent stained glass window, casting greens, reds and blues upon the wall.

"This is a wonderful house, Ramona." Carmen was truly impressed.

"It will be," Ramona answered. "I am lucky. We are lucky."

No dining table as yet graced the panelled dining room where a smoked glass table surrounded by steel chairs stood incongruously beneath a crystal chandelier, the table laid with supermarket delicacies of the early twenty-first century on white porcelain.

"Lunch first?" Carmen enquired.

"Lunch while," Ramona responded. "I lay the blame on Heinz."

"Poor Johnny. What blame?" Carmen asked.

"Well, first this idea of a celebrity wedding." Ramona gestured to Carmen that she serve herself.

"That was Maria's idea. Johnny's idea that we need profile, but Maria chose you. I was there."

"Well, it sounded like Johnny's idea the way he put it to us. Anyway, that's not what I mind. It's what he's put her up to now." Ramona's irritation was coming through and Carmen could feel it.

"What's that?" Carmen asked quietly.

"Oh, only to leak to the press, bit by bit, the whole story of our lives - you, me and Alistair - sort of before the launch of the film."

"Johnny would never countenance that," Carmen countered, relieved that it was nothing serious.

"Well he had dinner with her last night. First thing she does is call me up when she gets back in the middle of the night, all go, go, go." Ramona looked across stubbornly.

"So why didn't you tell her not to?" Carmen asked, surprised that there should be any contention between them.

"I did more than that, but she simply said I was foolish. My best friend, and she wouldn't even listen to me. I'm sending her an email, but I wanted to mention you in it, so I'd like you to see it. She likes you. Here, read it. Short and sweet, but true." Ramona slid a single sheet across to Carmen in a pink translucent cover.

"Thank you, Ramona. I shall not need my rose-tinted spectacles. But there's no story anyway, no evidence." Carmen started to read.

Dear Maria,
You are my best friend, and I yours. I am so close to the greatest thing in my life, and now I fear for it.
It is not just that: it is what welled up from within me after we spoke. I thought I was young and naïve when I left Alistair in Cambridge, but

now I know it was the same feeling, the same as when I heard of my sister, my as yet unborn sister. It is like a rage within me, and I did not admit it then, but I admit it now to myself; I did not reveal it then, but I reveal it now. And I think it is from something within me that I do not know, but what is missing for us.

Carmen broke off reading.

"You can't send that."

"But I must. Why not?" Ramona insisted.

"Because that is not how the world works, Ramona."

"You've been spending to much time with Heinz," Ramona stated dismissively.

"Then tell me what Johnny John Heinz would say, if that's what you think," Carmen responded.

Ramona thought about this.

"He might say, as a practical man, don't create evidence where there is none, i.e. the email."

"You underestimate him, Ramona. It would not get that far. He would say negotiate from strength, and this puts you in a position of weakness."

"Negotiate, Carmen? With my best friend?" Ramona countered.

"All relationships are negotiation, even from the little child that says, Mummy, I will only go to bed if you read me a story. But there's more, Ramona. Things happen in life that change relationships. We do things, strange things, for reasons we don't know. You: once my sweet little baby, now not even my friend. Why did I do it?" Carmen risked stating the truth, as she knew it, but did not wish to go further.

Ramona began to see a different perspective, though this did not help her to a solution. She felt her anger building, but could control it, and wondered what it was in Maria that could prompt her to this. Ambition? Jealousy even? Maybe she quite simply did not see the problem for Ramona? Seeing Ramona waiver, Carmen slipped the email from its cover, tore it into small pieces. Ramona could not help but laugh at the ignorance of tearing up the paper copy of an email, and Carmen blushed realising this. Always Johnny John Heinz now, Ramona thought, almost as if she is in love, but kept quiet, enough complications. A truce prevailed for the remainder of lunch.

As they sat over coffee, Carmen took her decision.

"I will help you with Maria," Carmen said. "And Johnny will help."

"How?"

"Give me the rest of the day to think, Ramona, and we'll talk tomorrow. I don't share your concerns for me, but I hope you will believe that I feel them very vividly for you, and for Mortimer. Don't talk to Mortimer. The solicitor's solution will just make it worse."

Carmen refused the offer of a lift to the station, preferring to take a taxi, now that the discussion was over. As she rode up Park Lane, she could not help but think how strange it was that everything was coming to a head at once. Suddenly the film, which had been in the foreground all this time, no longer mattered, for the moment, and yet it was the film that was the cause of everything, of all the changes that were affecting them.

When Carmen arrived back in Cambridge she was exhausted but confident. On the doormat lay mail, which she picked up and took through to the conservatory. First a coffee, she thought, and returned a few minutes later, such a beautiful room on these cloudless days. She always opened the strangest envelopes first, and as she read the contents of this one her confidence ebbed away. She reached for the telephone.

CHAPTER TWENTY-FOUR

DEUS EX MACHINA

Ramona

A surprising, seemingly urgent call from Carmen requesting that he come over; still, Johnny John Heinz was there now, but no one answered the door. Well she was expecting him, so he pushed the door open, stepping into the hall; glanced into the sitting room, empty; the study, empty; kitchen, empty. He walked down the corridor to the conservatory, and there she was, in a rattan seat, head back looking up to the clouds floating above the glass ceiling, in her hand a letter, an envelope discarded on the floor. She started as she heard him, and waved him into the room. She seemed distracted, even distraught, but seemed to draw strength at once from his presence.

"Thank you, Johnny."

"If I knew what for."

"You will."

She passed him the letter to read. She waited as he started to read, and then while he read she related to him her conversation with Ramona of the previous day. He finished the letter, placed it to one side, and looked up at her, with a frown.

"Complicated," was all he said.

"That's why I want to know what you would do, Johnny."

"Probably what you will, Carmen."

She thought about this for some time.

"Use my strength, Johnny, and I am a performer," she finally decided.

"Who will you play?"

"I shall be Inspector Poirot, Johnny. I shall take them all into the library. I shall use the little grey cells and reveal the plot. Poirot brooks no dissent."

"And the murderer?" he asked.

"There is none, not a murderer." Carmen closed her eyes in thought, continued. "Such a year, Johnny. Meeting Ramona, back with Alistair, Maria and the film. An exciting year, but just months: this year has not finished. It has much more, it seems, a wild year, taking its own course, uncharted."

"I take the point, Carmen." As much concern showed in Johnny's expression as in Carmen's.

"And then you, Johnny, these last days. I just invite you around to play the guitar, and you take on the film."

"Have it thrust down my throat." The Johnny John Heinz grin revealed itself, but only fleetingly.

"And now we really need you, Johnny. You are my *deus ex machina*, the god who descends to the stage at the end of a classical tragedy to untangle the affairs of humankind."

Johnny could not help but laugh at this metaphor.

Carmen continued, "We do need you, Johnny. Alistair doesn't, as always just resigned to it. Mortimer will, and Ramona. Maria needs you, Johnny."

"I hardly know these people, Carmen," Johnny protested.

"But I know you, Johnny." Carmen threw him a meaningful look. "You know what I see in your eyes, Johnny?"

"Tell me."

"I mean when you look at Maria. I'll let you choose, Johnny, choose the look you prefer me to see: the lost soul reaching out for paradise; or the ravishing beast held in check only by the bounds of modern society."

"You're a tough negotiator, Carmen. What do you want me to do?" The grin returned.

"I want you to be here tomorrow, but only once Poirot has concluded, to be there for Maria."

"And what's in it for me?" Johnny's confident laugh suggested to Carmen he was about to agree.

"That one kiss, the kiss for which you have longed all these year's, after which you may die a happy man." Carmen watched him with an air of defiance.

"Your kiss?" he asked.

"Johnny, really! My kiss, the kiss of Carmen, would breathe into you everlasting life, immortality. No, Johnny, Maria, her kiss." She paused. "I am relying on you to help us resolve this, Johnny, because I know you can, that you can be our *deus ex machina*, and if you are to be a god, then maybe I should bestow immortality upon you."

She moved across to him, leaning down, to bestow a lingering kiss upon him, and just as his instincts sought control, she withdrew.

"I'll call to let you know what time tomorrow, Johnny, and remember, you're now safe to accept that kiss from Maria, now you are immortal, and I have exacted your promise on that." As Johnny left, Carmen wondered how she would extract the one last answer she needed from Maria, the answer she wanted before they all met tomorrow.

Carmen had called them all. They all could come the next day, and now the next day was here and they had arrived. Carmen had wanted to speak to Maria since her arrival, to hear the truth, and had not - now the others were waiting in the sitting room. Carmen asked Maria to join her in the study for a moment. They stood opposite one another, Maria with an enquiring gaze, and still Carmen did not know how to broach the subject, and then she knew, thought maybe she knew, and she had to broach it, her last chance perhaps.

"Maria, I ... I don't know how to say this ... I'm, no ... Maria, how should I say?" She lowered her voice, almost in the back of her throat, "A lady of the blue sofa." Carmen stopped, but Maria looked at her blankly.

"I mean just once. No ..., I mean on one occasion." Maria put her arms around Carmen's shoulders, leaning towards her, so that Carmen felt her hair on her cheek, her breath, and gently in Carmen's ear, Maria whispered, "Same."

"Did he force you?" Carmen asked.

"It was, well, you sink back so gently, softly into that blue velvet sofa and feel so vulnerable, so exposed, well, Carmen you *know* how you feel, how *I* felt," she whispered. "Reluctant, no willing, willing him but hoping he would not, but that he would ... and he just stood there, and I was just so exposed ... and I think it was me, I think I invited him. He had choice, but for me choice was slipping away. I slid lower in that blue sea of a sofa and now I had no choice, and I saw that he stood there still, but I knew now he had no choice, we both had no choice. I could see in his eyes that he had no choice." Maria stopped and Carmen was silent. Maria continued. "Same, Carmen. One occasion. Never again."

So the secretary did respond truthfully to Alistair's questioning when he was down in London that day, Carmen thought. And Maria continued, still a low whisper in Carmen's ear, "And that is why I think I want the child: I could have stopped, could I? But I did not. And sometimes I lie awake at night and think that I want the baby to prove to myself that I did not do it just in the flush of approval of the film's finances, gratitude, but then why never again, Carmen? I only ever sat on that sofa one more time, and that was sitting next to Ramona; he was late. I told her the sofa was immodest. I could not stay on the sofa but went to the desk and there was a diary left to be read, a message for me, I think, and it said, *gentlemen do not talk.*" Maria put her arms around Carmen. And to herself Carmen said: my daughter, I must protect my daughter.

Maria whispered to Carmen, "Our secret is safe."

"There is no secret," Carmen replied, "You must simply deny it, deny it even to him. Come, let's join the others."

But Maria held Carmen back for a moment, raised her head, and said in a new firm voice, "But now I have changed my mind. When I look at a man like Johnny John Heinz, I realise my decision was wrong, and I shall change it. There is more, there can be more for me in life, and I do not wish to throw away a wonderful future."

"I think you are right," Carmen agreed, "Come on, they're waiting for us."

Maria felt relieved that everything had been set to rights now, was clear cut: Alistair and Carmen with their baby; Ramona and Mortimer; and her, Maria, and, just maybe, Johnny John Heinz, or someone else.

Then they went through to Ramona, Mortimer and Alistair in the sitting room, chatting, but clearly intrigued to know what this was all about.

Despite all the work on *Clunk*, this was the first time since that first film meeting in the Lanesborough Hotel at Hyde Park Corner that Ramona had been with Carmen and Alistair together. For reasons as yet unexplained, Carmen had wished that both Maria and Mortimer join what seemed to be some kind of special family event she was staging. As they took their seats, Carmen gravely turned, closed the door and then walked across to sit behind the desk, pressing a quick dial key on the speakerphone.

"There's a quirk in our family history," she said, as the speaker-phone dialled through. "It's contained in this letter. I thought it best we be together for this. In truth, I find it very, very hard. The letter arrived yesterday." The telephone connected.

Alistair, Ramona, Maria and Mortimer sat and listened in silence as Carmen read out in a clear voice the content of a letter she had received from a bishop in Spain. And in Spain, Clara listened in on the phone.

A hundred metres down the road, in the wings, Johnny John Heinz waited, unusually for him with trepidation, sadness, menace? He knew not what, but he would know soon.

CHAPTER TWENTY-FIVE

PRINCE OF THE CHURCH
SISTER CLARA'S STORY

Ramona

I, Clara, am now in my fifties, several year's older than my sister Carmen. Does wisdom come with age? As I sit in the courtyard, I realise that events have conspired to cause me more confusion than ever in my life before. Can this be? What is different?

I have learned that they, I mean Carmen and Alistair, now live together, and I am glad; I have learned that they will have a second daughter, and I am glad; the sun shines warmly upon me here as I plan my next steps in my new phase of life, and I am glad to be here.

My sister Carmen, the black sheep, the dark horse the unchained spirit. What is sin? This woman is to have a second child with Alistair, her one man, to whom she has remained constant all those years apart; this woman has taken hold of her destiny; she has honed her talents; she has fulfilled what it was hers to become. And she was the black sheep? What of me?

I have learned how Maria has grown close to them, but I must go back in time for you to understand what that means to me, for you to understand the decision I face. It is not the fault of my two brothers; no, they did more for me than anyone could expect, for me and not for Carmen, why not for Carmen? I am confused: I must be clear, as I always am.

I am addressed as Sister Clara, although I do not belong to an order: I was the principal of the school and therefore I was Sister Clara, a school with just twenty pupils and one teacher, me, in its last year and now no more. It was my life, and I suppose it is the life I chose and my brothers protected. Did Carmen need no protection? I suppose she did not: a black sheep needs no protection. Is that why she seldom contacted us and never saw us? She would know, or maybe she is just Carmen and would not know. Perhaps that is how we differ, Carmen and I.

This is a difficult path that I tread, after all the obstacles, then seemingly insurmountable, were crossed and left behind us so long ago. Ramona, what is the role that you play in this? I ask again, what is a sin? Is there that sin embedded deep within you like the flaw in a diamond, discerned as the rough stone is cut and polished? But it cannot be sin that gives rise to a jewel, my jewel. You do not understand, I must explain. There is little to be said, but that little has a density of mass. Where does it start? I cannot start at the beginning. Let me start where I can, and perhaps I can work back to the beginning. How can we have done this, my brothers and I? But we did. Perhaps we did this, my brothers and I, as much for Carmen as for me.

I gave her to the mad woman, with the help of my elder brother, who with his position and authority could achieve anything. It had to be the mad woman, who had no memory of her life since her youth, and therefore no story to tell, other than her ancient tales, over and over again. Did I want to tell *him* of the child, to tell him, a man of the church, the result of that one, that first, occasion? No. Sin? How can it have been a sin? I often wonder how things could have been different, but they could not. If not him, it would have been another, as it has been others with me, unlike Carmen who has only Alistair. Yes, it is true: I had a daughter by a bishop of the Church, and my brother the physician, a powerful figure in society was able to arrange to protect me and the family, and my daughter. Times were changing in post-Franco Spain, but this remained the only route available then, or let us say respectable route. And my bishop does not know, did not need to know, still does not know, does not know yet.

So what is different now? Well that is the real story. I loved that daughter and I still love her, even though I seldom see her now that she lives in England. She is talented and successful and I am a proud mother, and the mad woman has taken her secret, which she probably never understood, to the grave. But now I have a dreadful sense of foreboding. Now I really will go back in time for you and perhaps you will understand, or you may not. Who could?

When Carmen left her child, Ramona, with us, Fernando and I concocted the report to the police; yes now I think of it, really to protect Carmen. The child could stay with me and then, when it suited Carmen, she could take the child back, and the child's recovery could be worked into the kidnapping scenario, easily, based on the police reports in Seville of an unknown abandoned child.

I suppose we thought that Carmen, the black sheep, was in trouble and we had to keep her out of trouble, and in this case out of jail; with my brother's connections we felt ourselves to be above the law - he had fixed the situation with my daughter - and now Carmen was doing whatever she was doing, and we would fix that, from our end. It just seemed so like her to have let the situation escalate to this point (instead of coming clean at the time) ruled by passion not reason, and then she had even written that mad ransom note to herself and Alistair. The death of an unidentified couple on that same day in Seville added credibility to our story of the lost child, credibility that we did not need but accepted gratefully - we even had potential kidnappers on the file. We were young. Were we reckless? It all seemed so...so reasonable then.

But Carmen did not take the child back, and then in the late summer I went back to the police and told them how we had discovered, in the gardens of the Alcazar, that the child could speak English, but that simply helped to confirm my custody of the girl. The official version was on record. That obstacle was behind us. How one thing leads to another, one transgression to another! We could do anything.

I began to think it was wrong that my sister's daughter should live with me - I wanted her to live with her natural parents, Carmen and Alistair - and my daughter, whom I loved and missed, should live with the mad woman. And now it comes out, the truth, my truth: why should they not be switched? Carmen could always get her daughter back from the mad woman. There was a problem with the age difference of the two girls, just over two years, and that is why I moved the mad woman to a new place, to Rio Tinto where she was not known, to Rio Tinto where I did my charity work and could keep an eye on my niece. Did I worry of confusion in the girls' early memories? Did I worry that Carmen would find out? After what she had done?

Why did I never tell Carmen? Why should I? As the years passed, the difficulties slipped away, and today even the age difference can no longer be seen between my daughter, Ramona, and Carmen's daughter, Maria, which names are, of course, technically the other way round, as Romana is my daughter and does not know it. How could I have told her? Was I concerned when Ramona went to Cambridge? Not really, since I knew Alistair was not her father, and my daughter could look after herself. Did I like the book, *A Melody of Sadness?* I loved it: she writes so beautifully and she was writing of my sister, whom I always loved, even if she, the black sheep, had deserted us. Then the theft and publication of the book by Alistair killed any father/daughter prospects, which anyway I think there had never been. (Did he ever have the DNA test done? I think not). And when Carmen called Ramona from Buenos Aires after she heard about the prize? Carmen who had left her daughter twenty years before - surely no cause to be concerned about mistaken identity. Why should she not believe me, and when Ramona sang, it clinched it for her, but I can sing like Carmen too!

So what is my concern now, callous Sister Clara who has orchestrated this tangle? I hear that Ramona is angered by the thought of the unborn sister, who is not her sister but her cousin. I hear that Maria is working on a project with her mother, Carmen, who does not know Maria is her daughter or even that they are related, and then there is Alistair, the father, who was the most wronged of them all, both then and now. And what of early memories Maria may have? Will they be like dreams? Or will they surface? What have I done? Where will this lead? That is my problem. Is this sin? Sins not yet committed? Sins to be committed?

Catholicism is graced with confession and absolution: this story I have never confessed, nor expect any priest to believe. Will he believe me, my Prince of the Church, the author of my cardinal sin? I will enclose a copy of the book *A Melody of Sadness* with my letter and the published section of *Ramona*. The Prince of the Church must know whether Ramona is to learn who Ramona is, even who her father is, and if Maria is to learn that she is Ramona. My god, what have I done? Help me, my Prince.

Johnny John Heinz

The Reading Group
There had been no interruptions, and as Ramona spoke those last words, *what have I done? Help me, my Prince,* it was as if no one even breathed in the room. Fragrant air came in from the small London garden, accompanied by the gentle background hum of traffic and a distant police siren. It was Vera's house, and she did not know what to do. Should she clear away the teacups? That seemed wrong. She was stiff, undecided and did nothing.

So this was the autobiography of Ramona, but the writer was not Ramona, she was really Maria, and much of the life recorded was that of Ramona/Maria and some was of Maria/Ramona; well, however you are supposed to think about the characters now.

Pam opened, "I'm confused. I need to go back to chapter one."

Now that she was not first, Gloria could not wait, "Ramona, which is what I think we call you here, you've done it again, cut away the foundation. First the kidnapping that wasn't, then Alistair not writing the book, Mortimer in Romania and then not in Romania and now the virgin birth and Ramona."

"Have I," Ramona responded, "or has life?"

"I think life is asking for almost as much suspension of disbelief as art here." Vera had finally come to grips with the situation.

"Surely belief depends on perception rather than underlying reality," Ramona said, "The story changes because of perceptions, not facts. Imagine two stories. In the first, a lady falls off a bicycle hitting her head on the curb and suffering memory loss. The second is the same except that she was hit by a car."

"Inspiring stories, and?" Gloria was showing her irritation.

"Well," Ramona explained, "belief and understanding, *unlike reality,* depend on perceptions. Story number two *exists* only if someone else sees the car, as the lady with memory loss knows only that she lies next to a broken bicycle when she comes to."

"But what are you trying to say?" Pam asked with her newfound confidence.

"In reality," Ramona suggested, "the cyclist needs story

number two for her insurance claim, so she needs someone else's perception of events for the story to *exist*."

"Well, I imagine that *is* true," Vera said resignedly.

"Unfortunately, *reality* is not quite so simple: the insurance company disputes the claim saying she never learnt to ride a bicycle. Now that's what you're accusing me of today, but that's not what I did."

"I will confess that I am completely mystified," Pam said, which condition was shared by the other group members, "but I loved the book right up to the very last words. All those years ago and it comes back to haunt her."

"But there's still the Epilogue," Ramona said. "Let's see. It's Tuesday today. I'll email it to you before the weekend."

The mood was still thoughtful within the group, not yet ripe for discussion, so they agreed to meet up after the Epilogue, and after time for digestion of the work.

Vera took a deep breath. "Ramona, I know we have not yet finished the book, but I think this is the moment."

Ramona was surprised. "For what?"

"We have a present, to express our thanks," Pam said.

"We've been moved," Vera went on, "not just by the book, but by your being here. It's one thing to put matters so close to you, so honestly, in a book, quite another to be here in this small group. I know we've not always succeeded in keeping strictly to the book. I hope we have not caused you hurt by this, but anyway, once again, from deep down, thank you."

Vera embraced Ramona, Pam followed suit, while last, and possibly least, was Gloria.

Leave taking was strained and Ramona breathed a sigh when ten minutes later she was in her car and on her way back to Knightsbridge.

On and off over the next three days Gloria endeavoured to crystallise her thoughts, thoughts that revolved in her head in every free moment, mistrustful, angry thoughts, though she knew not why. It was late on Friday evening and Gloria lay back on her bed, cushioned by deep pillows, a glass of white wine at her elbow. She would try once more to draft her letter to Ramona. She had addressed her as Ramona and then crossed it out: she was not Ramona, but yes she was Ramona, and always had been even if she wasn't; well, she was

Ramona to Gloria. She started again. She wrote of how Ramona had first destroyed her perception of the book, *A Melody of Sadness,* with the knowledge that Alistair had not written it, rather she had, Ramona the daughter. And then Ramona had won them back with sympathy for her, for her life, her autobiography. And then on Tuesday they had learnt that Ramona was not Ramona. At this point Gloria ruined the next draft with tears, tears of sympathy or anger? Once again the ground had been cut from beneath them, but once again, surely it was Romana who deserved sympathy.

Finally, her rage abated, and she, tough hard-bitten Gloria, realised she was unfair to Ramona for all she had suffered and dared to record in a book, which she had read to them. Gloria's humanity won with the next sip of white wine. She screwed up the paper and decided the computer was a better bet - no more wettened and ruined drafts. Gloria poured her heart into the email to Ramona, effusive in her apologies, and simply clicked the send/receive button before prudence could second-guess the spirit of her note.

Gloria's email crossed with the promised Epilogue of *Ramona*, sent by Ramona Evans, which came up on Gloria's screen.

EPILOGUE

Ramona

At the weekend Ramona set off for Cardiff, first thing on Saturday morning. Spray from the motorway smeared the screen and big blue motorway signs announced those interminable miles ahead with irritating frequency. She clicked on the radio, a literary programme about her book, yuck. Well, there would soon be a furore. How should she play this? Should she really include the Epilogue? Get it over with?

In Cardiff she parked her BMW on the street in front of a row of terraced houses, somewhat out of place in this milieu. A black haired lady answered the door.

"Hi, Mum," Ramona said, coming through into the front room, where a man in his fifties sat and smoked a pipe.

"Hi, Dad."

"Ramona, it's been a while since you won the prize. Has it made you rich yet?"

"The book's already made me rich, Dad. Now it'll make me very rich. Read it."

"You must be joking, Ramona," her mother laughed. "Your Dad's not read a book since he went to school. I liked the bit about the rose in my teeth in your new book, *Ramona*, in Buenos Aires, performing in the opera. We haven't seen you for months, dear."

Ramona went through to the kitchen with her mother to have a cup of tea and talk about the new book, *Ramona*. You see it's all one big fraud really, she told her mother. Ramona had hoped for success, but she had never thought the book, *A Melody of Sadness*, would go quite that far. In Ramona's opinion Ian Fleming had just as much merit with James Bond as Shakespeare had with Macbeth, and maybe more: Ian Fleming had to create his character, while Shakespeare borrowed his from the historical record. Real literature is just a story, she told he mother. What some of these types do is try to read into it all kinds of other stuff. They look for underlying philosophical arguments, in vogue, or social commentary, human truths. What's that for a cannibal, or a nazi for that matter? My hero, the professor, is a very acceptable type, you know, academic, sensitive. Then we have Ramona, Andalusia, Europe moving from the traditional to the modern, the noble human spirit conquering adversity, and above all they think it's autobiographical."

"I like to think it is too, Ramona. It makes me very beautiful and romantic."

"Don't joke, Mum. They used to think some guy called Jamolla wrote the first book, but now they know it was a *nom de plume*. In the Epilogue to *Ramona* they're going to find out I'm just some Welsh girl, and that's after I've stung them with the whole Maria fiasco. The only thing remotely Spanish about me is the dark hair, oh, and the name."

"Blame your Dad. It was his idea at the time."

"The point is, Mum, the place will be crawling with reporters, inventing the truth. But if I put the real truth in the Epilogue, as I plan, then I think it'll be over quickly. I wonder if they'll withdraw my prize, when the entire fabrication comes to light, or if they'll say all the underlying truths were so brilliantly portrayed: a child of her times, subliminally, without knowing it." Ramona was interrupted by the ringing of her mobile, the caller's name on the display. She answered Gloria's call. A voice, immediately.

"Ramona, you've ruined everything for me. I believed in those people. Now I've read the Epilogue."

"Suspension of disbelief, Gloria, you know the phrase, we've had it before, I've just unsuspended you."

"But on Tuesday..." Gloria's voice trailed off.

"On Tuesday, you still all believed it was me, though you were a bit shocked by which one of the two was me, or rather who I was not. Just artistic licence again, Gloria, artistic licence." There was a silence, broken by Ramona.

"Tell you what, Gloria. I'll inscribe a copy, specially for you, minus Epilogue. How's that?" The phone went dead. Ramona looked at her mother.

"It's already starting, Mum"

"Ramona," her mother spoke thoughtfully, "that was Gloria calling about the Epilogue, so she's read the Epilogue."

"Yes, Mum."

"So Gloria..." hesitation, "what...I mean...what's actually *in* the Epilogue?"

POST SCRIPTUM

A HERO OF OUR TIMES

The vortex swept down from the Arctic, clipped the Urals and veered westwards, beating back the Atlantic weather systems, air-brushing pure white the land surfaces below, for East Anglia the heaviest snowfalls recorded this millennium. News reports were already coming in of motorists trapped in their cars, babies born in ambulances trapped in snow drifts, while the snow-ploughs ploughed and the grit trucks gritted.

The room was dimly lit by a couple of flickering candles and the light of the open fire, glinting on a Persian silver samovar, a haven of warmth from the fierce cold outside. Nestled at his feet, she gazed up at him where he sat, a faint smile playing on his lips. A tranquil scene they would remember forever, because in the next instant there was a blinding flash of white light, and for a moment the room plunged into darkness, and then came a sharp retort like the pop of a Champagne cork, which of course it was - even in Johnny's house Alistair would undertake this task as often as required.

"Well, that's the last picture on my film," Mortimer said, "and maybe the best." He smiled down at Maria. "That wonderful expression of sheer adoration. You should be in the films. And you, Johnny, I congratulate you, probably the first person ever to have his novel ghost-written by the winner of the literature prize." Alistair poured the Champagne and Johnny accepted the toast with grace, and then suggested they switch on the lights. In the corner of the room a Christmas tree sprang to life with its reds, yellows and greens pulsating, before Mortimer discovered the button to switch them to constant mode. Mounted on the wall Johnny's collection of silver gleamed almost white and the brass items took on the yellow glow of gold. The weather raged outside, so that even Cambridge would no longer be accessible that night, not even with cross-country skis.

"This has been a wonderful evening and a marvellous dinner, Johnny." Carmen was full of praise. "When I asked you to help us, I knew you were inventive, I didn't know what to expect, but this, Johnny, what can I say? Where did you get the idea?"

"Actually the idea came to me in what can best be described as illegal circumstances, on the bike, the M11, conforming to what everyone takes to be the speed limit, eighty-five miles per hour. Then with a flick of the wrist, these bikes are amazing now, in less time than it takes to crop the end of a Havana cigar, you've doubled your speed. So there I am racing past these people who'll probably tell their grandchildren about it, listening to Radio 4 in the headphones."

"What!" Ramona interrupted. "You listen to Radio 4 at a hundred and seventy miles per hour!"

"There's nothing wrong with Radio 4, Ramona. Anyway, they're talking about the cost to the taxpayer when the judge ends a trial, orders a retrial, because of stuff in the press that might colour a jury's view. So then I think, and I know it doesn't really work like this, Mortimer, so don't correct me, what if we colour everyone's view in advance. Then you can't have a trial because you won't find an unbiased jury, except I decided to make it a bit more complicated than that, and I'm talking trial by press, not the legal variety. And then I thought, why not roast two birds in one oven? One, kill any investigative forays into the wicked past before they start; and two, publicise *Clunk*."

Alistair laughed. "Well, Johnny, after reading Ramona's book, sorry your book, I don't think anyone would believe a word they read in the Sunday papers on the subject, and neither can I see a police investigation into Carmen. They'd be laughed out of court, no pun intended."

"And isn't that amazing? Virtually everything we wrote was true, except the fiction about Cardiff and Ramona being Welsh in the Epilogue," Johnny answered.

"So what's the publicity bit?" This is what interested Maria.

"There are several parts to this, Maria, but first let me be brash." Johnny looked down at Maria, and a softness came into his eyes.

"Maria, if you'll take me as your husband, we'll have a double wedding with Ramona."

"Johnny! There are others present!"

"Please, Maria, family, just witnesses, no jury."

"I will, I mean, I do."

And Johnny bent down to her to applause. Maria rose and sat next to Johnny, who placed an arm around her.

"You interrupted the proceedings, Johnny, continue," Maria said, a flush on her face, a desire to hide the tumult within her.

"Publicity. *Clunk*. Well, Carmen is going to sue me for libel, Ramona is going to sue me and my publisher for plagiarising *A Melody of Sadness*, Maria is going to sue me for the sex scenes, and Mortimer, when interviewed, is going to stand aloof, claiming it is all too trivial, beneath him, and yes he rather wished it were true, having seen pictures of Maria in the gutter press."

"Are you going to be able to afford all this legal stuff, Johnny?" Alistair asked.

"For a professor of literature, you can be very literal sometimes, Alistair," Johnny answered. "We'll settle out of court before we even get to court. This will be the cheapest publicity campaign a film has ever had."

"And probably the most notorious," Carmen added.

"And the whole press interest will stem from Ramona, because she's famous, and she'll go to her literary critics, claiming this is the most outrageous thing that has happened to an author in history. Everyone will want to read the book as well. Injunctions? Well, I'm having it printed in Slovakia, so they can't even go through the European Court to stop me. Don't correct me, Mortimer, just a manner of speaking."

Johnny took Maria's hand and stood, she rising beside him. He turned to Mortimer.

"That image of Maria and me on the last picture of your film, taken just now, will be with us forever, Mortimer, thank you." He kissed Maria. "And now for the sensation, the sensation of the decade, headlines, the coup de grâce for the evil monster."

"Johnny, you're too much of a ham to make it in films. Get on with it," Carmen instructed.

"This is what we're going to do, as far as the world is concerned.

During the negotiations for the settlement out of court, the ruthless corrupt Johnny John Heinz falls in love with the gorgeous, innocent, wronged Maria, whom we by now all know so well from her pictures in the papers. Heinz and Mortimer become firm friends, playing in the same polo team. We all know that Mortimer is marrying Ramona. And then at the height of the *Clunk* campaign, the news leaks, news that no one believes: there will be a double wedding. The press battle rages, until reluctantly Mortimer confirms that it *is* true, but requests respect and privacy, as the paparazzi snap away. The wedding takes place to catch the Sunday press in the week before our première." The famous Johnny John Heinz grin was dispensed to the room, but it was with dismay that Maria looked back at him.

"I thought you *did* love me, Johnny."

"And I do," he reassured her. "I have always combined business with pleasure, but have never had an opportunity such as this in my life before, I mean in all respects." He paused. "But I'm a sly one. If you had refused me, everyone by this point in the proceedings would have understood my proposal differently. No loss of face for Johnny. So that's it. In mathematical terms sesquiplicate."

Outside the arctic winds remained oblivious to Johnny's machinations, but within the room there was complete silence, as each of them considered the magnitude, the deviousness, the outrageous aplomb of Johnny's plan. It was Carmen who broke the silence.

"All I expected of you was to rescue our family, our relationships, from their strange circumstances and you conquer the world." And then she added, "I'm speechless," heading in the direction of the oxymoron since she patently wasn't.

There was a metallic clang, reminiscent of centuries before, as the clock on the mantelpiece struck the first stroke of midnight, followed by the second, but at the third stroke it stopped with a kind of clunk. They all looked at the clock.

THE END

OTHER BOOKS

BY

JOHNNY JOHN HEINZ

MEANS TO AN END

Enter the world of money laundering, financial manipulation and greed, where a shadowy middle eastern organisation takes on a major corporation in the US. As the action shifts through exotic locations, who wins out in the end? Certainly, the author's first hand experience of international finance lends the plot chilling credibility.

THE SIGNATURE OF A VOICE

The Signature of a Voice is a cat-and-mouse game between a violent trio, led by a psychopathic killer, and a police officer on suspension. Move and countermove in this chess game is planned and enacted. The reader, in the position of god, knows who is guilty and who plans what, but just as in chess, the opponents' plans thwart one another. The outcomes twist and turn to the final curtain fall.

To order additional copies of Ramona and other books by Johnny John Heinz please visit: www.twentyfirstcenturypublishers.com

Printed in the United Kingdom
by Lightning Source UK Ltd.
1301